Matched For Love

Rocky Mountain Matchmaker

TAMRA BAUMANN

To Jan,

Hope this brings you
a smile.

Tamra Baumann

Text copyright © 2017 Tamra Baumann
Published by Tamra Baumann
Cover design by: Clarissa Yeo
Printed in the United States of America
Matched For Love

Tamra Baumann

Dedication

This book is dedicated to my critique partners, Robin, Sherri, and Louise. You ladies make my life brighter. Thank you for all you do for me!

1

BEING A SINGLE MATCHMAKER ISN'T NECESSARILY GOOD FOR BUSINESS.

Lori Went wished she had a clone. Or the money to hire a housekeeper, a handyman, and a cook. Being a single mother was a challenge she hadn't signed up for. Lately, she felt like the roadrunner in those cartoons competing against that wily coyote, running all the time, destined for nowhere in particular.

Shivering from the January cold, Lori jogged beside her daughter through the doors of the busy cafeteria at Emily's school in the burbs of Denver. The science fair was in full swing, and they were late.

As usual.

Emily looked a little pathetic holding her project, or what was left of it, as they searched for their assigned spot. The box top holding clear plastic cups filled with her daughter's lima beans in various stages of growth had spilled some in the car. The sprouts lucky enough to have survived leaned a little like drunken sailors. And Em hadn't finished gluing on the result cards per the instructions. Hopefully they could hurry and do that before the judges came by her table.

Thankful for her height, Lori peered over other heads and finally found Emily's name card. When they got to their table and she saw the complex project next to Em's spot, she pulled up short.

Emily's face lit up. "Look, Mom. We're next to Asher and his dad! Hi, Mr. Cooper."

Asher's dad, Deek Cooper, glanced Lori's way and sent her one of his panty-melting smiles. "Hi, ladies, great to see you again."

"Hi. That's an impressive display, Asher." Lori tried to keep the sigh from her voice. Em's project looked a little lame compared to that.

Deek nodded. "Asher worked really hard on this." Pride for his son shone in Deek's big smile. The pure joy on Deek's face made her lips tilt too. Deek was a nice guy, and all the kids loved him.

Asher's dad was also the perfect "class mom." He claimed to have time to help because he worked from home designing video games or some such. Whatever he did, he was very successful and donated tons to the private school both their kids attended. To top it all off, he was the preferred chaperone for all field trips because, apparently, he was fun. He was an amazing single parent and always made her feel a little inadequate.

But really? Could a second grader, all on his own, create a display showing how the first personal computer came up with its answers? Asher was a bright kid. Maybe he *had* done it all by himself.

That thought made Lori feel even guiltier than she already did. She should have spent more time with Emily on her project. But when would she have fit that in? She had her matchmaking business to run so she could pay the bills her military widow's benefits wouldn't cover, along with trying to keep up with her on-line accounting degree classes. There weren't enough minutes in the day.

Deek bent down to Emily's level. "Wow. This looks awesome, Emily. Good job!"

The man was a super cute, gym built blond who wore T-shirts with funny sayings, and jeans most of the time. The shirt he had on showed a picture of molecule rings, and it said: *Never trust an atom, they make up everything.*

Despite her harried day, it made her chuckle.

She'd always appreciated the way those silly T-shirts stretched across his big chest, and it *was* appropriate for a science fair, but really? It was the dead of winter. A button-down flannel would've been more appropriate for the snow still falling outside. But then, he could probably afford the best coat money could buy.

The blond, blue-eyed mini version of Deek, Asher, scrunched up his nose. "Your plants are kinda crooked, Emily."

Emily looked up at Lori and shook her dark-haired little head in censure. "You drive too fast, Mom."

When Deek cringed, Lori wanted to crawl under a rock.

"I'm sorry, Em. Let's see if we can fix them up." Lori started to take one of the more pathetic plants from Emily, but Deek beat her to it.

His hand, surprisingly rough for a computer programmer, brushed against hers as he accepted a cup from Emily. Then he glanced up and said, "You need to go check Emily in at the registration table." He turned his focus back to Em. "How about I give you a hand until your mom gets back? The winners go to regionals, right, guys?" Both Asher and Emily nodded. Asher much more enthusiastically than Em. Probably because he had an actual chance to win.

"Oh. Right. Thanks. I'll be right back." She *knew* Em had to be registered. What was wrong with her lately?

Lori shook her head at her forgetfulness and shrugged out of her coat as she weaved through the kids and parents preparing their displays for the judges. When she got to the registration table, her friend Shanan was standing in line. Lori leaned over her shoulder and whispered, "You're late too, huh?"

The petite brunette turned around and rolled her eyes. "Got two at home puking up their guts with the flu. Then my mom was late to sit with them. I was just trying to decide what's worse, science fairs or visits to the gynecologist. At least at the gyno, I can lie down for a bit and get some rest."

Lori loved her friend's sense of humor. "Did you see Asher's display? I don't think *I* could have come up with that, much less Emily."

Shanan laughed. "Asher got his father's smarts, but really? I told Deek he's making us all look bad. He actually *made* the cupcakes for the winter party from scratch. Who does that anymore?"

"I know, right?" Lori's cupcakes had been sort of home-made, though. Her friend Jo had made them. Jo's café was still under construction from a fire, so she'd offered to help Lori out. "But Deek is sweet to the kids, so I guess I'll give him a pass. Has he ever asked you out?"

"No." Shanan finished signing her daughter up and then stepped to the side. "He's so damned cute, I asked *him* out, but he said he's tired of pointless dating. Maybe he just wasn't interested in me, but in case *you're* interested in him, he's off the market. He's going to try to work things out with Asher's mom. She's some archeologist who never comes home. She uses the computer screen to visit with Asher now and then, I guess."

How sad is that?

Lori stepped forward and greeted the volunteer, then got busy signing up Em. "I'm on Deek's team. I'm not interested in dating right now either." She wasn't ready to move on from her husband.

That, and learn to trust again. Having a father and a husband who cheated made it hard to think about putting her heart out there again. She'd found out Joe had cheated on her—with her former best friend—right before he'd been deployed, so they'd never worked their feelings out fully. Then he was killed, so they never would.

Never was a long time.

"It's been two years, Lori. You could be like me and just date for fun. It doesn't have to be a long-term thing that messes with your heart." Shanan studied the number card in her hand. "Do you think 666 is a bad sign?"

Lori laughed. "It's just a number. But speaking of numbers, when are you going to start letting me give your number out to some of the *nice* guys I have all picked out for you? Those men you're dating are just using you for sex."

"You've got it backward. I'm using them. I'm basically going to act like a player until I get it out of my system, then we'll talk. But you're not wired like me, so it's time to use your matchmaker skills on yourself and get back out there. We're not getting any younger, you know."

"True." Lori sighed. Thirty-three wasn't *that* old. Was it? "I'll think about it. But back to you and Deek. Maybe things won't work out with his ex, and you'll finally be ready to settle down by then, so it could be a win-win. Don't rule him out. Friends fall in love all the time."

Shanan shook her head. "Deek probably just isn't attracted to short, big-boobed, brown-haired women with three kids, but was too nice to say so."

"You're a doll. So I know that's not it. And it's been almost two years for you too. It'd be the ultimate revenge on your cheating ex to be in a happy relationship."

Lori felt a little hypocritical saying that when she wasn't moving on, but she believed in the truth of her words…for everyone else. She had bad choices in men running in her gene pool. Look at her poor mom. She'd picked the wrong guy too.

"I suppose." Shanan shrugged. "But for now, I'm happy to just look at Deek when we volunteer together. The dreams later that night aren't too shabby either. See you after for yucky punch and stale cookies?"

"Can't wait." Lori made her way back to Em with her number in hand, dreading the judging that was about to come. Pizza at their favorite place for a consolation dinner probably loomed in their near future.

When she got back to the table, Deek was busy using a glue stick and fixing up the poster board for Emily's project. The rules said parents shouldn't help, but Deek wasn't Em's parent. After he had finished his magic, everything looked tidy and neat and not nearly as sad as when they'd first come in.

"Thanks, Deek." Now that she knew he was safe and not going to ask her out, she wanted to repay him for his kindness. "Would you and Asher like to grab some dinner at Papa G's with us after?"

He glanced her way and blinked as if he was surprised she'd asked. They'd known each other for over a year, and she always enjoyed talking to him, but they'd never shared a meal before. So she quickly added, "Just as friends, of course. Not a date or anything."

Relief crossed his face, and that sexy smile of his was back. "We'd love to, right, Ash?"

His son, busy repotting one of Em's plants, nodded. "Yeah. That'd be good."

"Great. Then it's a date." When Deek's blue eyes cut her way again, she said, "I mean it's a non-date?" She lifted her palms in frustration. "We'll go eat after?"

"Sounds good." Deek returned his attention to making Emily's science fair project judge ready.

๛

Deek breathed in the aroma of garlic, red sauce, and juvenile sweat that hung in the air at Papa G's pizza parlor. It was a noisy, fun place for kids. Since theirs were both off feeding the machines tokens while they waited for their pizza to come, he'd have to hold up his end of a conversation with a beautiful woman. Lori was way out of his league. Tall, built, dark-haired beauties like her always made him a little tongue-tied.

Drawing a deep breath for courage, Deek pulled out a chair across from Lori and settled in, hoping for once he could manage not to be awkward while eating dinner with a woman.

When Lori grinned at him, his heart rate spiked. Showtime.

She said, "Thanks for all the help with Em's project. Science stuff would've been my husband's forte. It's certainly not mine."

Should he comment about her dead husband? Was that bad form? Man, he hated small talk. "It was no trouble."

That was a lame response. He wished Annie would just change her damned mind about them and come home so he wouldn't have to go through the torture of having dinner with single women.

Lori had said it wasn't a date, though. He needed to relax and act like he was having pizza with one of the guys. "I mean, I was the biggest math and science geek there was in school. I enjoyed helping Emily."

"You were a geek in school?" Lori's eyebrows lifted. "I'd never have guessed that."

He nodded. "I was skinny, gangly, had glasses, and everyone copied off me whether I liked it or not. The kids called me Derek the geek, and eventually, it morphed into Deek. They called me that for so long, I didn't think to change my nickname when I went to college."

Lori's green eyes danced with amusement. "I think it's a great nickname. And you're hardly gangly now."

"My dorm mate in college took mercy on me. He showed me the wonders of the free gym privileges that came with our tuition. And how to hide my geekiness in public. I only geek out now when I'm home. It's the only place I still wear my glasses too." He was babbling and should shut up. "Was that too much information?"

"No." She took a sip of her iced tea. "And since we're confessing our at-home quirks, ever since my husband died, I started wearing yoga pants every day. He hated them. But now I have ten pairs."

The tension drained from his shoulders. Lori was easier to talk to than most attractive women. She'd always been nice, and he honestly liked her, so why had he been nervous? "I'm all for being yourself, especially at home. And you look very nice tonight, even though those pants probably aren't as comfortable as yoga pants." Lori wore a pretty blue sweater and gray slacks that showed off some impressive curves. But maybe he shouldn't have said that? Crap. Did he just put his foot in his mouth?

Lori's right brow popped up. "Thank you." She glanced in the kids' direction. "They should be running out of tokens any minute." She kept her gaze diverted from his.

He *had* put his foot in his mouth. "That wasn't a pickup line... I mean." He closed his eyes and ran a hand down his face to compose himself. When he blinked his eyes open again, he said, "I should just apologize in advance for the dork I can sometimes be. You and I usually talk about school stuff or our kids, but personal things trip me up. I never know how much to share. It's why I hope Annie, Asher's mom, will come back home and finally marry me. We're both giant nerds and meant for each other."

"No worries." Lori's smile returned. "So you were never married to Asher's mom?"

"I asked. But she has big dreams she wants to fulfill before she settles down. I can understand that, I guess. But I grew up without a mom, and I don't want that for Asher. It's why I stopped dating. My heart just wasn't in it. Asher would be better off with Annie."

He hated that Asher only talked to Annie once a week if that. If they spent more time together, surely she'd bond with her son and make them a cohesive family.

He really needed to figure out a way to convince Annie she loved him enough to come home. Being himself certainly wasn't doing the trick.

"Yeah. I hear you." A slight frown creased Lori's forehead. "I should probably try to date again. Find a man who'd want to make a family with Em and me, but I'd need one who came with a no-cheating guarantee. I wish there were such a thing."

He did too. He suspected Annie was attracted to another scientist on the dig. His name came up way too often. She'd always avoided commitment and liked keeping her options open. "My mother ran off with a guy and never looked back. I'd never do that to a spouse, much less my kid. But then, what did I do? Went and fell for a woman who loves archeology more than us." He was a top-notch programmer, won awards left and right for his mad skills, made more money than he could spend, yet he couldn't figure out how to get Annie back.

"So you're trying to woo her via the internet?" The pizza showed up, so Lori thanked the kid who brought it and then stuck two fingers in her mouth and whistled for Emily. The sound was so loud and shrill, her daughter looked up, grabbed Asher, and headed for the table.

The whistle impressed the hell out of him. Who'd think a classy woman like Lori would do something like that?

He mused so long that he'd almost forgotten to answer her question. "Yeah. It's tough dating on the computer. But maybe if I could whistle like that, her heart would be mine."

Lori smiled. "I could teach you how to do it."

"I might take you up on that." It wasn't the only thing she could probably teach him. He'd recently heard Lori was a matchmaker.

Deek silently ate his pizza while mulling over the pros and cons of asking Lori for some help to get Annie back. She'd probably be able to give him some tips to appear more attractive. But would that make him look like a suck up to Annie, who knew him so well?

By the time he'd worked out all the angles of asking the mother of one of Asher's schoolmates and friends for help, Lori stood to throw the trash away. "That was awesome as always. But it's a school night, so we better run."

He nodded around his last bite. "This is one of our favorite places too." He turned to his son, who'd borrowed Emily's cell phone. He was busy playing a video game. "Right, Ash?"

Asher's blond head just nodded in response, so Deek snatched up the phone and handed it back to Emily. "This is why you don't have one of these, Asher. You turn into a zombie when you play."

Lori had returned and slipped into her coat. "Sorry about that. Emily's uncle Nick spoils her rotten. He gave her that phone without asking me. But aren't you a video game designer?"

"Yes." He stood and slid into his coat too. "But we have strict rules about when we can play in our house." He leaned closer to Lori and whispered, "Lucky for me I can call it working." He hitched his eyebrows.

He'd always geeked out for hours on games every day since he'd built his first computer in the second grade, but he didn't want his son to be a nerd like him, so he monitored Asher's video game and TV time closely.

Lori nodded. "Convenient." She leaned down and held Em's coat for her daughter to get suited up for the brisk night as well. "I intended to treat you guys tonight. Next time, I'll need to be sneakier and beat you to the check." She stuck her hand out for a shake. "Thanks for dinner. It was fun. Good night."

"Our pleasure. Night." Afraid his hand might still be greasy from the pizza, he wiped his palm on his jeans first and then shook her soft, warm hand. He wasn't expecting the zap of heat that her touch sent straight to his gut. He held her narrow palm and long fingers as he analyzed his body's reaction. It wasn't static electricity. The only thing he could conclude was that it was pure lust for Lori.

She blinked in confusion at him and hadn't let go of his hand either. She must have felt it too. Weird. But nice. Interesting they both reacted to a simple touch.

It occurred to him that he was holding her hand hostage, so he quickly let go. As pleasant as that had been, he needed to stay focused. Keep his eye on the goal.

Win Annie back for Asher.

2

THERE'S NO I IN TEAM.
BUT THERE'S NO TEAM WITH JUST
ONE PLAYER.

Lori lifted the warm, steamy mug of coffee in her hands and drew in a deep breath. Nothing better than Jo's coffee to start her morning. Then she found a table in the corner of Confections and Coffee, Shelby's under-construction café, and waited for her sister-in-law to arrive. Jo, Shelby's business partner who was supervising the installation of an oven in the rear, gave a quick wave. Jo was Shelby's best friend and had become a good friend of Lori's too.

Lori and her sister-in-law had once been competitors in the matchmaking business but were now partners, thanks to her meddling brother, Nick. It had been the best thing her bossy baby brother had ever done for her.

The café was Lori's favorite place to hang out during the day to work on her classes and matchmaking business because she was always surrounded by her two favorite things: coffee and sugar. Even though the café wasn't open again yet, Jo always provided extraordinary baked goods each day for the workers. Actually, the baked goods were probably for Shelby and her pregnancy cravings, but either way, Lori benefited too.

At home, too many things stared at her and begged for her attention. Why she'd ever thought buying an older home with sturdy bones to fix up was a good idea was beyond her. She used to love to refinish wood, paint, and lay flooring. She'd remodeled two houses with her husband. They'd made some decent money flipping them, but on her own, it just wasn't nearly as fun. Instead, it'd become a little overwhelming, just like the rest of her life lately.

As she pulled her laptop from its case and shrugged out of her coat, thoughts of blond-haired, big-shouldered Deek Cooper filled her mind again. The way he'd helped Emily with the glue stick had been oddly endearing. And since when had a simple handshake been sexy? There had only been one other man she'd ever been so instantly, physically affected by—her husband, Joe. It was disconcerting. And a little bit thrilling. Deek had awakened deep desires within her she'd worried might be gone for good after her husband died.

But Deek was on a mission to get his ex back, so she needed to put her lust-starved thoughts aside. Not easy to do when it'd been so long since she'd slept with a man. Maybe it *was* time to use her matchmaking skills on herself, as Shanan had suggested. But first, she needed to get her economics home-work done. She hated that class, with all the terms she had to memorize. Especially when her brain was still tired from her lack of sleep the night before spent thinking about touching Deek's hand.

A few minutes later, Shelby flopped down across from Lori, saving her from production functions and isoquants. Shelby was short, blonde, and as cute as a button—even more so pregnant.

Shelby leaned closer to be heard over the drilling noise. "How's my *favorite* sister-in-law today?"

"Seeing as I'm your *only* sister-in-law, I know you're just buttering me up for something. How are you feeling, by the way?" Even at four and a half months along, Shelby still battled morning sickness.

"Like a queasy cow." Shelby grinned. "Did you see we got two new applications last night? One of them is perfect for *you*."

"Ah. There it is." Yesterday, Lori would have blown that statement off. Maybe she'd have a look. She pulled up their web page toolbar and found the applications. "Which one is it?"

"It'll be obvious. I'm going to go see what Jo made for us today." Shelby rose to check out the brownies and banana bread Jo had left on the counter. Lori had been tempted but decided she'd skip breakfast and wait to make that her lunch. Calories were calories no matter if they came from a sandwich or something yummy. She'd substitute the good stuff and go light on dinner. Keeping her figure was a full-time compromise.

Thinking of food reminded her that she'd had a craving for Chinese takeout for days. Maybe she and Em could splurge on that later.

Ignoring her empty stomach, she paged through the applications. The first guy was handsome but fifty-five, so she skipped to the next one. Bingo. The guy was thirty-six, tall, dark, and very good-looking. He had a big smile and was fit. Movie-star handsome, really.

She read his bio. Jason's family owned car dealerships, he adored kids, liked to hike, sail, Jet Ski, was a foodie and loved to read. He preferred women with fun personalities and who enjoyed eating. The last part was Lori to a T. She adored food. She just hated all the exercise and meals she had to miss because of it.

Jason might be a good segue back into the game.

Shelby returned with two brownies and two slices of banana bread.

Lori held up her hand. "Thanks, but I'm waiting for lunch."

With a brownie halfway to her mouth, Shelby said, "This is all for me. So? What do you think? Jason is hot, am I right?"

"Yes. Very." Lori saved both applications and filed them away. "But we don't know what his type is yet. Maybe he prefers short blondes."

"Nope." Shelby stuffed banana bread into her mouth next. "After I spotted his application last night, I knew you'd like him, so I sent him your picture. I wanted you to have first shot before we added him to the database. He's busy this Friday, but he'd like to have dinner with you the next Friday night."

"I don't know if I'm quite ready to date again." Lori stood to avoid the puppy-dog-begging-for-a-treat expression on Shelby's face. "I need more caffeine to make this big a decision."

While pondering, Lori ended up in front of the brownies. She successfully avoided temptation and poured herself more coffee. While taking a long sip, she hoped the caffeine would hit fast and give her some clarity. And maybe a little courage too.

Was she ready to date again? She had to get back out there sometime if she didn't want to end up all alone in a house with fifteen cats one day. Not that she had any cats now, but she'd always had a soft spot for kittens.

She'd sworn after Joe had died she'd never marry again. Or choose the wrong guy and get cheated on. Her trust issues were deeply seated. Watching her mother deal with her father's cheating had just made her even more reluctant.

But eventually, Emily was going to leave, and Lori *would* be alone. And then she'd be even older, and more set in her ways. Nope. If she was going to do it, it needed to be sooner rather than later. But then, maybe springtime would be a better time to start. New beginnings and all that.

Lori glanced at the brownie her hand had snatched up of its own accord, and then put it back. Just thinking about dating again obviously made her want to stress eat.

When she returned to the table to tell Shelby she wasn't quite ready to take the next step; her phone dinged with a text. She read the screen and sighed. "Emily is running a fever. The school nurse said she had ten kids in her office, so could I please hurry."

Shelby nodded as she finished off the last of her brownies. "Go. I can take your twelve thirty appointment."

"Thanks. I owe you one." After she'd gathered her things, Shelby stood and grabbed Lori's arm.

"No worries." As her sister-in-law dragged Lori toward the glass doors, Shelby said, "I'll tell Jason yes to next Friday. That gives you a week and a half to find the perfect dress. See you later." With one last shove, Lori found herself standing in the cold air on the snowy sidewalk.

Pregnancy had made Shelby a whole lot pushier. But maybe that was just what Lori needed to convince her to jump back into the dating game again.

Hopefully, it wouldn't be a disastrous date.

Deek tugged on the school's front doors. Of all days for Asher to be sick. Deek rarely had meetings with clients in person. They happened online mostly, but his biggest account had flown in a contingent of executives and designers to meet with him just for the day. They'd rented a conference room in a downtown hotel and were catering in lunch to save time. They wanted to bang out the details for their highly anticipated fall launch. They weren't happy campers about the interruption.

He needed to get back to his clients, but what would he do with Asher? Deek's dad wasn't well enough to take care of Asher on a typical day, much less when he was sick.

Damn Annie. It was times like this that he resented Annie and her decision to ignore that they had a son who needed them both. She never had to miss work or take Asher to doctor appointments or soccer games, or… He should stop. It didn't help to moan and groan about it. Asher was just going to have to come back with him to the hotel. If luck was with them, maybe this strain of flu wasn't a barfing one. Just the high-fever kind.

That reminded him that he'd have to add a stop at the drug store and grab something to treat Asher's fever too before he got back to work.

He hurried down the shiny hallway with classrooms lining the sides and arrived at the main office. There must've been six moms gathering up their sick kids. One of them was Lori. She glanced up and waved.

Suddenly, he didn't feel so alone in his quest. She knew what it was like to be a single parent too, and somehow just knowing they were both going to have screwed up days made him feel better.

"Hi, ladies." He glanced at Lori's daughter, whose cheeks were flushed with fever. "Sorry you're not feeling well, Emily. Asher seems to have the same thing."

"Thanks." She wrapped her arms around Lori's waist, hugging tight. Not at all like the outgoing girl Emily usually was. Asher probably felt just as bad.

Guilt washed over him for even thinking of taking Asher back to the meeting with him.

A slow smile lit Lori's face. "You clean up nice."

He'd actually worn a suit. And a tie. The importance of the meeting dictated he drag himself to his closet and make an effort. T-shirts and jeans were so much more comfortable, though. "Big meeting today. The Universe of Zeldane is at stake. But you didn't hear that from me. Highly hush-hush until next fall."

"Got it." She made a zipper motion across her full lips that was oddly sexy. "Asher is just inside. He was worried about interrupting you on your big day. I could watch him if you need some help."

Asher had seen the suit earlier and asked if Grandpa had died. The only other time Asher had seen Deek so dressed up was at Annie's parents' funeral. So he'd had to explain his important business meeting. But would Asher think Deek was abandoning him? "If I let you help me, would that make me the worst parent ever?"

"No. I already own that title." Lori waved a hand. "Besides, what're two sick kids when you have one already? Can Asher take ibuprofen?"

"Yes. He's not allergic to anything as far as I know." He ran a hand through his hair as he considered. Lori was obviously a caring mom. "Let me ask Asher." If his son freaked, he'd just suck it up and tell his client he had to reschedule. He'd probably lose the account, but there were others. Not many he wanted as much as this one, but his kid had to come first. "Be right back."

Deek squeezed through the gathering of parents bundling up their kids and met the nurse. He signed his name to check Asher out of school and then found his son sitting in a row of chairs. One of the last kids remaining. "Hey, buddy. Sorry it took me so long. Ready to go?"

Asher nodded and then slid off his chair. He held out a hand to hold, which Asher rarely did anymore, and it made

Deek feel even worse. The kid was really sick. He should just cancel his meeting.

When they found Lori and Emily in the hallway, Lori held her arms wide, and Asher slid right into her embrace. Maybe he should have hugged Ash. Deek's father never hugged much, so he wasn't sure by the second grade if guys were supposed to do that still.

Lori murmured softly, "I'm sorry you don't feel well, sweetheart. Want to come home with us? I have Popsicles, and we can watch cartoons or movies. That way, your dad can finish up his meetings and then pick you up after. How does that sound?"

Asher looked up. "I can go with Emily, Dad. I'll see you later."

"Okay. If you're sure." Deek felt like a horrible father. But Asher was in good hands. Although he didn't usually let Asher watch many cartoons. It'd probably be okay for just one day. "Lori, can we exchange information? I'll do my best to move things along and get him as soon as I can. I really appreciate this."

"No problem." She started digging in her giant purse for her cell.

After they typed in their data and swapped back, he said, "I'll call and check on you guys in a few hours, okay?"

"We'll be fine." Lori pulled stocking caps onto the kids' heads. "Good luck with Zeldane. If they serve Chinese take-out there, bring us some."

"Um. What?" He blinked for a second as he processed that. Had Lori meant bring takeout for dinner? Annie always accused him of being way too literal. "But the kids—"

"Will have chicken noodle soup and crackers if they get hungry. I have plenty of that. Chinese takeout, not so much. Knock 'em dead, Deek."

"Okay. But what do you like?"

Lori turned and walked down the hall with the kids in tow. She called out, "Surprise me."

"Yeah. Will do. Call if you need anything." He stuffed his hands into his pockets and watched them go. Surprise her? He hated when women said that because inevitably, he always got the surprise wrong.

❦

After a hugely successful, if not a bit rushed, meeting, Deek was armed with bags filled with Chinese food. He texted Lori from his car to apologize for being so late. It was almost eight.

Be there in ten minutes. Sorry!

No problem. I'm buried on the couch under two sleeping kids, so don't knock and wake them. I'll unlock my front door with my phone for you now.

Okay. See you in a few.

Deek tucked his phone away and then headed for Lori's house.

After he had parked in her driveway, he gathered up all the bags and navigated Lori's snowy walkway. He stomped the snow from his shoes, then stood before the front door of Lori's vintage Craftsman-style home with its cool, modern electronic lock. It felt weird to let himself in, but she'd told him to. He walked slowly inside and then softly closed the door behind him.

Lori's living room was big, with lots of wood accents. There were splotches of different colored paint on the walls as if she was deciding which she wanted, and all the furniture was under plastic drop cloths. The wood trim had been painted over years ago, but a few spots were uncovered and polished up, just enough to see the beautiful home it had once been. Lori must be in the middle of a remodel.

He continued walking down the long, wooden-floored hallway toward the high-pitched sounds of animation, and found everyone in the den. Lori sat in the middle of a large couch with her feet next to a laptop on the coffee table, her head leaned back, and her eyes closed. Both kids' heads were in her lap, and their bodies flung out opposite ways. Extracting her without waking them could be tricky.

But the way Lori's hands lay protectively on Asher's and Emily's backs as they napped sent a bolt straight to his heart. He'd never had anyone soothe him like that when he'd been sick as a kid.

He needed to get Asher his mother back.

3

DESPERATION CAN LEAD TO MAKING NEW FRIENDS.

Rustling sounds from the kitchen woke Lori. Must be Deek. Her empty stomach was thrilled their dinner had arrived.

She slid her hands under Emily's and Asher's heads and slowly wiggled out from under them. Gently, she laid their heads back down on the couch cushions and then tiptoed her way to the kitchen. A pair of suit-clad legs stuck out from under the kitchen sink. She knelt down to ask what he was doing and tapped a knee.

Deek's head shot up, and he bashed it on a pipe.

Her hand flew to her mouth. "So sorry. I didn't mean to scare you."

"That's okay." He winced and then got back to tightening the pipe. "I noticed you were in the middle of working on this, so I thought I'd finish it up for you. As a thank-you for watching Asher."

While wearing a suit? "Thanks. It was leaking a little, so I was just going to—"

"Rewrap the plumber's tape. I figured that out. Almost done."

"I would've never guessed former nerds with high IQs were good at plumbing too. You might come in handy yet."

"Maybe you'd better wait to pass judgment until we see if I fixed it." He slid out and then stood and turned the water on. They both leaned down, side by side, and waited for a leak to appear. When the pipe stayed dry, she gave him a shoulder bump. "Awesome. Now let's eat. I'm starving." She washed her hands, and then Deek did the same.

It was sweet of him to fix her pipe. She hoped they could become better friends. She'd enjoyed sharing pizza with him the night before.

Lori grabbed some plates while he unloaded the bags. Little white box after little white box appeared on the faded yellow countertop. The bag was like Mary Poppins' purse, filled with an impossible number of items. "Should I expect a football team to show up at my door any minute, or are you training to be an Olympic swimmer? There's enough to feed a small town."

He stopped unloading and cringed. "I didn't know what you'd like, so I just bought one of everything."

Lori smiled as she unwrapped pairs of stuck-together wooden chopsticks. "I'm not all that picky when free food shows up at my door, Deek. But thank you. I appreciate it." She started to pour them both glasses of water. But then for the heck of it, she grabbed a bottle of wine and poured out two glasses. "Did you happen to get any gong bao chicken? That's my favorite. Well, that and sweet and sour pork."

"Yes." His face lit up. "Those are my favorites too."

After they had loaded up their plates, they settled across from each other at the little round table in the nook. Deek asked, "So, how are the kids? Are their fevers any better?"

Her mouth was full, so she shook her head while she swallowed. "Both running about one hundred two. I think we'll probably have another sick day tomorrow. Did you get all your business taken care of?"

"Yes. Thanks to your heroic efforts today, the Universe of Zeldane will defend and defeat the massive invasion from the warriors of Trithor—if the gamer is clever enough. Thank you for saving my contract today. In your honor, I'm going to add a princess to the game and make her look just like you." He paused for a drink of his wine. "Wait. Did that sound creepy? I didn't mean it that way. If you'd rather I didn't—"

"No. I'm actually a little flattered." She'd googled Zeldane when she'd gotten home. It was the name of the highly antici-pated next installment in one of the most popular video games on the market. "Just make sure I have a fortified castle, so I don't get killed off. And give me a big closet filled with Louboutins. It's only fitting for an imaginary princess like me. Real-life Lori has never owned a pair."

"Those are the shoes with red soles, right? I went out with a woman once who asked me to buy those for her almost weekly. Then one day I overheard her talking on the phone to a friend. She admitted that she liked that I have a lot of money much more than she liked me. Apparently, I was too much to take sometimes. I didn't even see that one coming. I'm not always the best with social cues." He took a bite as he seemed to ponder that failed relationship. After he had swallowed, he said, "But you, princess-who-defiantly-wears-yoga-pants, will have complete editorial control over the closet."

"I'd expect nothing less for the use of my name and like-ness." She took a bite of the best sweet and sour pork she'd ever had. "Wow. Emily and I are going to have to go back to this place. Everything is awesome. Or am I just so hungry, my taste buds would think cardboard was good right now?"

"It's always good. And they're even open late. Annie used to crave it when she was pregnant with Asher. I made so many late-night runs that I'm now on a first-name basis with the owner."

Lori smiled inwardly as she sipped her wine.

How sweet was that? Joe hadn't been home most of the time she'd been pregnant. It would've been nice to be pampered a bit.

After a few minutes in comfortable silence as they chowed down their delicious food, she asked, "Any progress on the get-Annie-back front?"

He shook his head. "She was supposed to call this afternoon. Every Wednesday, I have to text and remind her, but I was so busy today, I forgot. I hope Asher wasn't too disappointed."

"He didn't mention it if that makes you feel any better." Sad that Annie didn't make Asher a priority.

Lori considered for a moment. A guy who admitted to not reading people well could probably use a little help getting Asher's mom back. "Maybe you should stop reminding her. I used to remind my husband about things all the time until I finally realized he had no reason to remember important things regarding me because I did it for him."

Deek grabbed his empty plate and took it to the sink. "I'm not following."

"He relied on me, but then because he did that, it made me feel like I was being taken for granted. And it was my own fault." She joined him at the sink and began loading the dishwasher.

He handed her his rinsed plate. "That makes sense. But I can't do that to Asher."

"I get it. I used to make excuses for Joe to Emily too. He liked to play golf on his few days off rather than spend time alone with his toddler. He said he never knew what he was supposed to do with her. And if I was there, he didn't see the need for both of us to have a ruined day off."

"Ouch." Deek turned and leaned back against the counter. "You let him live after a statement like that?"

"Oh, I let him have it, all right. But then, you can't change other people, can you?" She sighed as she loaded the dirty lunch and breakfast dishes from earlier into the washer too. "Joe was so clueless sometimes, but I loved him. And Emily figured it out anyway. She took it in stride as Joe just being Joe. Kids are smarter and more resilient than we give them credit for."

He crossed his arms as a frown formed. "When I was debating what to do with a sick kid today, I was thinking how crappy it is that Annie takes no responsibility for Asher. I'm going to call her when I get home tonight. Lay the law down, you know? Either she comes back, or…"

"Or, what? She's Asher's mom. It's not like you can break up and never see her again like you did the Louboutin woman. Don't go in hot. I know you're frustrated, but it'll just make things worse. Take it from a hothead like me."

"So Princess Lori has a temper, huh? That'll make for a better character." He leaned down and whispered, "Maybe I should make you one of the hot warrior women instead?"

When a slow, sexy smile formed on his lips, her stomach clenched. He was so damned good-looking. And the guy didn't even know it. That made him even sexier to her.

She whispered back, "No, thanks. I'd rather have those shoes." She should lean away, but he smelled so good, she didn't want to. The yummy aroma of leather, wine, and sexy man wafted from him.

What was she doing? He wanted someone else. She leaned away and broke their staring match. "So, do you want another glass of wine?" Liquor was the last thing her libido needed, but she couldn't come up with anything better while he was looking at her like that. She needed to tamp back those formally dormant urges that were raging like a wildfire inside her. Deek was not available. She understood that in her head, but her hormones weren't listening. She needed to go on that date with Jason. Maybe if things went well, she'd be able to bury her deep-seated physical desire for Deek.

Deek wanted another glass of wine, but he better not. Lori was way too easy to talk with. Besides, she'd looked away and seemed uncomfortable all of a sudden. Or maybe he was just boring her. "Thanks, but I better get going." He laid his empty wineglass in the dishwasher and then headed for the den to gather up Asher.

"Thanks for a great dinner, Deek. And for leftovers to last a week. Do you want to take some along?" Lori trotted along beside him, and her smile was back. Probably relieved he was finally going to leave her alone.

"Nope. You earned them. Anytime you need a sitter I'll return the favor."

Her forehead scrunched. "Well, actually, are you busy on Friday night next week?"

"Yeah. I mean no, I'm not busy." He hefted his sleeping kid off the couch. "You have a big date or something?"

She nodded. "I do." Then she crossed her arms and frowned like Asher did when he wasn't thrilled about doing something.

He wasn't sure why the thought of her going on a date didn't sit well. That she didn't seem happy about it made him feel better, but it was none of his business. And he owed her a huge favor

"Then I'm your man. Maybe I'll take the kids to eat and then we'll go to that new place that helps them write their own book if that's okay?"

"That'd be great. Emily has been bugging me to take her for weeks. I'll send some money along."

"No. You probably saved me from losing hundreds of thousands of dollars today, so it's my treat." He headed for the door as Asher snoozed on his shoulder.

She stopped dead in her tracks and blinked up at him. "You make that much money making up games? Maybe I should switch my major." She ran ahead of him, grabbed Asher's coat from the rack, and then opened the front door.

Crap. He shouldn't have said that. That was the second time he'd mentioned money in the last ten minutes. Now he'd never know if she was being nice to him for his wealth like so many other people in his life. That was why he needed to get Annie back. She'd never cared much about money.

He took the coat Lori held out and wrapped it around Asher's shoulders. "Text me what time I should pick Emily up next Friday."

Lori shivered in the cold air the open door let inside. "You don't have to go out of your way. I can drop her off at your house."

He'd sworn he wouldn't let another woman see his three-million-dollar home either. Not until he was sure he wouldn't get used for his money again, at least. "It's no trouble. It'll be on the way."

Lori hugged her middle to stave off the cold. "Okay. I'll text you that afternoon. Asher can have something for his fever in a half hour. Good night."

"Thanks. Night." He carried Asher to the car, wishing for his own coat he'd left on the front seat. Asher finally woke up a little, making it easier to strap him in before he fell right back asleep. Then Deek slid behind the wheel.

It was later than they usually talked, but maybe he'd call Annie anyway. As he headed for home, Deek ran words around his brain to say to Annie to convince her to come home after her dig finished. He needed to stay calm like Lori suggested, and just lay out the facts. That ought to work better with Annie, because she rarely lost her temper, outwardly, like he did.

After they were home and Asher was tucked into bed, Deek picked up his cell to video chat with Annie. She was supposed to be on her short break and back in her meager living quarters for the week before she went back to the field.

Finally, after five rings, she answered, rubbing the sleep from her eyes as she walked down a hallway. Away from her bedroom's closed door. "It's late, Deek. What's wrong?"

He wanted to ask if she remembered she was supposed to have called her son but refrained. "Nothing. Asher was sick today, so I forgot to text my weekly reminder to call. Sorry about that."

"I can't believe I forgot. We've just been so busy here. I'll try to call tomorrow. Is Asher okay?" She frowned as she sat on an old couch in the living room.

Wait. Why would she have gotten out of bed? His stomach sank as possibilities rushed into his head. "Do you have company?"

"Yes." Her head tilted to the side. "But I don't understand the upset expression on your face, Deek. We both agreed we could sleep with others. It doesn't mean anything. It's just sex. You've been with other women since I've been gone."

"Not since we decided we'd try to make our relationship work, three months ago. I thought no sleeping with others was implied." He felt like he was going to be sick.

Annie's blue eyes just stared back at his as she processed his words through that damned logical brain of hers.

Her blonde hair was rumpled too, and he didn't want to think about how it'd gotten that way.

Finally, she said, "I'm sorry. I guess I misunderstood our agreement. But we talked about this, remember? You should sleep with other women, Deek. That way we'll be sure when it's time to settle down. Right?"

He'd been sure since she'd become pregnant. It was his responsibility to marry her and be a good father. "Wrong." Hot anger welled in his throat, but then Lori's voice in his head reminded him not to lose his temper. "What it's time for is for me to show you what you're missing. We both know that, empirically, we're a perfect match on paper. You've just forgotten it. Now go kick that guy's ass out of the bed I paid for. I'll call you tomorrow. And every day after that until you remember why you used to love me."

"I —"

He quickly disconnected the call before she could disagree with him. She'd said she'd loved him once. Maybe she'd been a little drunk at the time, but it'd been enough for him. It'd been the only time *anyone* had ever said the "L" word to him, beside Asher, so he remembered it distinctly.

After tossing his phone on the coffee table, he stood to pace. His gut ached at the thought of losing her. He couldn't let that happen, for Asher's sake. But what could he do to win her back that he hadn't already tried? He needed some big-time help.

Maybe Lori was still up. He scooped his phone from the coffee table and started to hit dial, but stopped. He didn't want to wake Emily. He texted instead. *9-1-1. Can I hire you? Annie had another man in her bed when I called just now.* He stared at the phone, begging Lori to see the text. After a few minutes, she replied.

Yikes. That's not good. But you don't have to hire me. I'm happy to give you some tips.

I insist. I'll even pay double if you help me figure out what I'm going to say when I call her tomorrow. And every day after until I win her back. I don't know why I said I'd do that, but now I have to come up with a bunch of clever crap to say to her.

I charge four times my usual rate if I have to come up with CLEVER crap. But because we're friends, I'll cut you a break.

Relief washed over him. For the help and because she still thought of them as friends. He hadn't been sure when she'd seemed so uncomfortable earlier.

Thanks. But if I do dumb stuff to annoy you, please just tell me, okay? I need your Princess Lori powers to save my kingdom and keep it intact.

A few moments passed with no reply. Had that been a stupid thing to say? Had he just messed up what he was trying to save with her? He should have just said thanks and signed off for the night instead of being such a geek.

Sorry. Emily woke up. She needed more medicine. Asher does too, by the way. And I'll be sure to let you know if your nerdy super brain annoys me, Obi-Wan Kenobi. But now I have to go. Talk tomorrow?

Sounds good. Thanks.

Don't forget Asher's medicine :0)

On it. He tossed his phone aside and then went to the kitchen to get the children's pain reliever.

He heaved out a long breath as he headed up the stairs to Asher's room. Hiring Lori was a good plan. It'd work.

It had to.

4

COME TO THE DARK SIDE—WE HAVE COOKIES. AND CARTOONS.

At three o'clock on the dot the next day, Deek and Asher stood on Lori's doorstep. Deek wore an open coat that showed off his T-shirt that said: *Always give 100%—unless you're giving blood*, and Asher was bundled up appropriately for a sick kid. She opened the door wider in invitation.

"Hi guys. Come in."

She closed the door after they trooped inside and hung up their coats on the rack by the front door. "How's the appetite today, Asher? Are you hungry for a snack?"

Deek answered, "He hasn't been hungry all day. But whatcha got?" When he grinned, she couldn't help but smile right back.

There was something so hot and yet so innocent and kind about Deek. He looked like a macho, tough guy build-wise, but then all sorts of goodness just radiated through his gorgeous turquoise-colored eyes. Annie was a fool to let him run loose in the wild. Some smart woman was going to snag and bag him soon if Annie didn't hurry up and come to her senses.

"Emily said she wasn't hungry either, so I was forced to dig out the secret weapon from my rusty arsenal. I baked chocolate chip cookies."

Asher's face brightened. "Yum."

Deek's brows drew together. "I try to limit Asher's sugar intake, so we only have cookies on special occasions."

Lori led the way to the den where Emily was watching an animated movie. "Then you guys are in luck. That I actually baked *makes* this a special occasion. How about just one?" She glanced over her shoulder to get Deek's permission. He stood with his hands on his hips, scowling at what was playing on TV as if it were porn. "What?"

"I'll be right back, Asher. I need to talk to Lori in the kitchen about something." Deek slipped his large hand around her waist and gently tugged her against his hard body. He whispered, "They watched cartoons all day yesterday and now one of those silly animal movies?"

His hot breath on her ear was warming other parts of her and made it hard to concentrate. "If it makes you feel any better, they were both so sick that neither of them even cracked a smile yesterday. It was embarrassing when I was the only one laughing."

As Deek continued to guide her to the kitchen, she added, "That was a joke, by the way. I probably only really laughed out loud once."

They got to the kitchen, and Deek quickly released her as if he'd finally realized she'd been snuggled against his side. He lifted his hands in frustration, but then let them drop to his sides. "Fine. He can have one cookie. It's just that we have rules in our house, Lori."

Like she didn't?

She crossed her arms. "Rules are essential. But I don't see anything wrong with making an exception when they're sick. Are you this strict with Asher all the time?"

Deek ran a hand through his thick blond hair and stalked to the table in the nook. After he had dropped into a chair, he said, "Maybe I'm a little hard on Asher, but I don't want him to end up like me. That's all."

Lori's irritation with him instantly vaporized. "Hold that thought while I slip your kid some sugar crack. Be right back."

When she returned to the kitchen, she laid four cookies onto a plate and poured them two glasses of milk. "Hurry and explain what you meant before Asher's brain cells melt out of his ears from watching top-notch animation with a thoughtful message."

When she set a glass of milk and the plate in front of him, Deek snagged a cookie and took a big bite. "Sarcasm and I don't always mix. Are you saying I'm just being mean?"

"No, I don't think you're being mean. I respect that you're careful with Asher's sugar intake. I watch Emily's too. But I don't understand why it'd be so bad if Asher turned out like you."

Deek finished off the first cookie and then his hand dove for another. "You should bake more often. You're very good at it."

"Now you sound like my mom. She thinks I should cook homemade dinners for Emily every night like she did for us growing up." She took a bite of the still slightly warm cookie and moaned with pleasure.

After a slug of cold milk, she continued, "I justify my behavior by telling myself I'm expanding Emily's palate whenever we occasionally grab things like takeout Thai food. And grilled cheese counts as a full homemade meal if you add fruit on the side, right?" Lori finished off her fourth cookie of the day and weirdly didn't care about the calories for a change. They were damn good if she did say so herself.

His cookie stopped halfway to his lips. "I cook for Asher most every night. So what does that make me?"

"Dead. If you tell my mother. Now quit avoiding my question about Asher and answer, please."

He leaned back in his chair and crossed his muscled arms over his chest. "I used to be on my computer so much as a kid, that it became my only passion. So I regulate how much TV, computer, game playing, and reading he can do in a week. I don't let him get obsessive about just one thing. He's smarter than most his age, so I encourage him to join in with normal, more popular friends like Emily. That way, he won't have to endure all the teasing and name-calling I had to put up with."

"Normal?" Lori tried to refrain, but her snark regulator had been out of service lately. "Are you implying that my kid isn't as smart as yours? And that Asher is lowering himself somehow by being Emily's friend?" She spoke in a clipped tone but wasn't really mad. Asher was the smartest kid in Emily's class. Everyone knew that. And Emily wouldn't be a boy's friend unless she honestly liked him.

Deek opened his mouth, but nothing came out.

She quickly added, "Maybe what makes Emily so 'normal,' as you put it, is because she watches channels other than just PBS, and is pretty obsessed with soccer at the moment. She sometimes plays video games after her homework is finished too. I like to think she's well-rounded, Deek." Lori rose and grabbed the cookie jar. She laid it on the table between them and sat down again. "Want another? Or do only geniuses have enough restraint to eat just two, unlike us normals?"

"Sorry." Deek held out his hands, palms up as if surrendering. "I didn't mean it like that. I just..." He shook his head. "See? I manage to make a mess of all my friendships. Maybe I should go."

When he started to rise, she held up her hand. "Stop. I'm not mad at you. I'm only pointing out there might have been a better way to say what you wanted to say. You might be super smart, but what you just said was pretty dumb."

He slowly slipped back into his chair. "So which part was the dumb part, exactly?"

"Pretty much all of it." Lori snagged her last cookie of the day and took a bite. "Saying your kid is above average and then calling others normal could be insulting to some parents. And in my humble opinion, there's nothing wrong with kids being passionate about things they enjoy. We'd never have professional athletes, or great musicians, or painters if everyone thought like you. Would you be as good at your job today if your father had squelched your interest in computers?"

"I don't know." Deek shrugged. "My father barely knew I existed while I was growing up. He only notices me now because I drop off a check when I visit him once a month to be sure he's taking care of himself."

"I'm sorry to hear that." Lori gave his forearm a quick squeeze before putting her hand back in her lap where it belonged—in case it decided to explore that sexy forearm on its own. But that Deek grew up that way hurt her heart. "It's an even greater testament that you're such a great father, then, Deek. After having Asher here all day yesterday, I can tell you he's very well behaved and polite… Wait! Is that why you volunteer so much at school? So you can see how he's interacting with the other kids?"

"Busted." He opened the cookie jar and grabbed another.

"Okay, all that volunteering in class and trying to be the perfect parent has to stop. Mostly because it makes all the other parents hate you a little for doing it so well."

He grinned. "Now that you know my secret, I have to stop, or you'll think I'm obsessive about it, right?" Deek finished off his cookie.

"Exactly. And maybe if you watched some of the movies, you'd see they're pretty great."

"Okay. I'll try to have an open mind. Text me a list of the better ones, and I'll preview them for Asher."

"Will do. Ready to start Operation Get Annie Back?"

"Yes." He reached for a piece of paper in his back pocket. "But before we start, I wanted to show you the mock-up of Princess Lori I drew this morning."

She accepted the paper from Deek, and her jaw flopped open. "Geez, Princess Lori is much sexier than me." The cartoon character looked very much like her in the face, but her boobs were two sizes bigger, her waist was teeny tiny, and her hips curved in a much more enticing way than Lori's real ones did. Jessica Rabbit had nothing on Princess Lori. And she wore a very low-cut dress that showed off more cleavage than she could ever wish for. "Could I borrow that dress for my date next week?"

Deek slid his chair around and settled beside her as he studied the drawing. "I think this looks a lot like you. Just enhanced a tad to make it a good characterization. But sadly, I don't think I could whip up that dress for you that soon."

Lori turned her head and met his steady gaze. "If you tell me a guy with as many muscles as you have can sew too, I'll have to smash my 'Best Mommy in The World' mug over your head."

"Then for safety purposes, maybe I'd better not tell you about a certain person I knew in college who had to make his own medieval cosplay outfits because he was so broke."

"Nope. Better not." It made sense that a guy who designed video games would be into dressing in sexy leather and brandishing swords. The image in her head was making her have naughty thoughts about Deek again, so she picked up the cookie jar and put it back onto the kitchen counter to put some space between them.

She was starting to understand why her friend Shanan enjoyed gazing at Deek when they volunteered together. And like her friend, the spicy dream that would probably come to her that night would be torture. In it, he'd probably be wearing warrior gear while ravishing the much-sexier-than-her Princess Lori.

Brother. Even in her dreams, she wasn't getting any action.

Her date with Jason couldn't come soon enough.

Deek munched another cookie while having a hard time keeping his eyes off Lori's ass. He wanted to win Annie back, that was the goal, but he couldn't help where his mind had wandered while he drew Lori earlier. She had a body with real curves. He'd never had a girlfriend who'd been shaped like that. The few he'd had were always stick thin. Her figure intrigued him, that's all. It wasn't like he would ever be disloyal to Annie.

Like she'd been to him.

How could she have told him to sleep with other women without even a flicker of emotion crossing her face?

Yet those same carnal thoughts about Lori had come rushing back while he'd watched her check out her character a moment ago. It didn't help that the yoga pants Lori wore made her rear end enticing enough that any guy would have a hard time not noticing it. He wished she'd sit back down, so he didn't have to *keep* noticing it. "I went over the ideas to win

Annie back you e-mailed to me earlier. I can't decide which way I want to go. I really liked the going to virtual counseling together, but she'd never go for that."

Lori turned around and leaned against the countertop. "Well, if that's the case, I'd like to see you and Annie interact, to get a better idea of your relationship dynamic. Can you video chat on my computer? That way we can also transfer her image onto the TV in my bedroom. I can stay out of sight, but watch too."

"Sure. We usually call around this time, so I'm ready whenever you are." He was going to be in Lori's bedroom? Just pile on the temptation.

He grabbed Asher, who protested loudly about having his movie interrupted, on his way through the den, and they followed her hot behind to the bedroom. It was all very... girly inside. Tons of throw pillows on the bed, pale yellow walls filled with pictures of Emily with a man who must've been Lori's husband, Joe. The air even smelled feminine. A combination of flowers, citrus, cookie dough, and Lori. Super enticing.

After Lori got the television synced up, she held out a hand toward her little desk in the corner. "Here you go. Just to be on the up-and-up, tell Annie I'll be in and out, so she knows I'm here too." She handed him a piece of paper. "After Asher is done, we'll let him get back to his movie in the den, and then you and Annie can talk." Lori put her hands over Asher's ears and whispered, "That's a list of *clever* crap to say if your conversation stalls. Some of it's kind of spicy."

Lori had all the bases covered. He was in good hands. He made the connection to Annie's computer, then he sat Asher in front of the screen. When Annie answered, Deek told her that Lori was there too and then went and stood beside Lori and watched their interaction.

Annie looked tired, but nodded and listened while Asher told her his news.

After Asher got done telling Annie about all the cool movies he'd been watching and the cookies Lori had made, Annie frowned slightly. "Why would Deek let you do that?"

Dammit. This isn't going to help my case for getting her back.

Asher shrugged. "Because Emily does all those things? Or maybe it's because Dad likes Mrs. Went. He made her a pretty princess in his game. And he even made her a castle."

"Deek made her into a princess?" Annie blinked a few times as she considered. "He's only made me a warrior who lives in a tent."

Lori made a choking noise next to him.

He whispered, "Maybe I'd better go put a stop to this."

"Wait." Lori laid a soft hand on his forearm to stop him. "Making her jealous might work. Let's see what she says."

"She's not jealous. Just last night she told me to date other women."

Annie said, "Regardless of why, I'd prefer you didn't watch cartoons and eat sugary sweets, Asher. Those things aren't good for you, sweetheart." Annie leaned closer to the screen. "Where are you, exactly?"

"In Mrs. Went's bedroom. It smells like flowers in here."

That got a reaction out of Annie. Her brow creaked up a half inch. "Okay. Where's Deek?"

"Wait, Mom. I wanted to tell you about my science fair proj—"

"I'm sorry, Asher, but I'm late for something. I promise I'll hear about it next time. I have to go. But I need to talk to Deek first."

When he started for the computer, Lori whispered, "If she told you to date, then maybe it wouldn't hurt to make her think you listened."

"I've never lied to Annie."

"You don't have to lie to her. Just imply." Lori's warm breath against his cheek as she whispered sent a punch of desire straight to his gut.

When he turned to gaze into her eyes, her lips were so close, that he had to lean away, fearful he'd do something dumb. Like, kiss her. "Are you sure?"

"Yes."

He didn't know if he liked the idea of implying things, but then, Lori was the expert. He wasn't getting anywhere with Annie doing things his way. "Okay. But stay. In case I start going wrong, will you?"

"Of course." She patted his arm. "You got this."

He exchanged places with Asher in front of the screen. After Asher had gone back to his movie, Deek said, "Hey, there."

"Hi. What's going on with you, Deek? Are you okay?"

"Yeah." He shrugged. "What do you mean?"

"Yesterday you got upset that I'm sleeping with someone else when I know we hadn't agreed to monogamy. Then you told me you're going to call every day. While that's nice, you know I have limited time to talk. And now you're letting Asher run amok, while video chatting from some strange woman's bedroom? You're being…inconsistent."

Letting Asher run amok? It took all his self-control for him to remain calm. "It's not a stranger's house. It's his friend Emily's. The other television is being used by the kids. And for future reference, Asher has told you about Emily many times."

Annie shook her head. "What does a television have to do with our video chatting on a computer?"

Crap. Why had he mentioned the television? He glanced Lori's way. She held up a piece of paper that said "ignore the TV," and she'd written what to say next. He turned back to Annie. "Are you mad about the princess and castle thing?"

"No, not at all." Annie blinked rapidly again. "It seems strange, that's all."

He read the next sign Lori held up and then asked Annie, "Don't you want to come home and be a family again?"

"Eventually, of course." Annie waved a hand. "Which might be soon if we don't get the next round of funding. You could help with the money, you know." Annie sent him a tired grin.

His hopes rose at her lack of funding. "Nope. Asher and I need you here. The sooner, the better."

Annie chewed her bottom lip. "I'm doing real work, Deek. I thought you supported my career."

Lori waved another sign to get his attention. It said, "I need your help with something ASAP! Hang up."

Confused, he said to Annie, "Lori needs something. I'll call you tomorrow." He hit the disconnect button and then asked Lori, "What do you need?"

"I needed your help making her jealous. I asked you to say that so you wouldn't have to lie. Get it?"

"Ah." He chuckled at how obtuse he could sometimes be. "That was smart."

Lori sank to the side of the bed, leaving about an inch of clearance between both their knees. "Does she always call you Deek in front of Asher?"

He nodded. "She thinks labels and titles are overrated."

"Oh." Lori leaned closer. "Anyway, she seemed a little upset with you. We need to keep poking at that in the future. Jealousy is a strong emotion."

"I wasn't sure if it was that, or because I refused her the money for her dig. She's asked me for funding before."

Lori laid a warm hand on his thigh. "Don't take this wrong, Deek, but any woman who would use you for your money is one you don't want. Even if she *is* Asher's mother."

Lori glanced at her hand and quickly moved it as if his leg was on fire. "You deserve someone who loves you just the way you are. Goofy T-shirts and all."

She'd grinned when she mentioned his T-shirts, so she was probably teasing him about that part. But she'd seemed serious about the rest. "I know Annie loves us. She's just super busy, and she shows love in her own...way."

"Okay." Lori shrugged. "I'm not judging. Only trying to be a good friend."

"Thanks. I appreciate it." Annie wouldn't do that.

Lori just didn't know Annie like he did. That was all.

5

GETTING BACK IN THE SADDLE DOESN'T COME WITHOUT ITS ACHES AND PAINS.

L ori stood before the floor-length mirror in her bedroom and frowned at herself. Should she wear the sexier blue dress instead of the more classic black one she had on? The thought of her date with Jason had made her sick to her stomach all day. It was either that, or she was catching the same flu the kids had the week before. It could be a plausible excuse to get out of her date.

No, she needed to pull the trigger and get it over with. Joe's death was no reason to bury her life too.

She laid a hand on her rounded stomach and drew a deep breath. Why had she made irresistible cookies right before her first date back in the game? She'd probably had fifteen in the last week, dammit!

The doorbell rang and made her jump. Deek was going to sit with the kids, who'd decided they wanted to watch movies and play video games rather than go out.

Good. She needed a male opinion.

She was getting entirely too used to seeing Deek every day. When she refused to take money for her help with his daily

Annie calls, Deek suggested he help her around the house for a few hours each day. They'd made some major progress with the painting and the sanding the past nine days in a row. The guy even worked weekends. And he looked so hot in a tool belt, that she'd found him jobs just so he'd wear it. And when he'd whipped off his shirt to rub it in her face after she'd started a paint fight, she'd practically drooled over his six-pack abs.

She'd begun to look forward to his visits way too much. So much so, she'd even started wearing jeans instead of yoga pants, and putting on makeup. But Annie had insisted earlier that he stop calling so often because she didn't have time to chitchat, so her daily dates with Deek were going to end. She wished he had a clone. She'd go on a date with that guy in a heartbeat.

She rushed down the hallway and opened the front door. "Hi, Asher. Emily is in the den. Deek, I need your help in the bedroom." She grabbed Deek's hand and tugged him down the hallway.

"Just to be clear, it's probably too much to hope you're dragging me to your room to ravage me instead of making me fix your sink again, right?"

Deek was joking. He wanted Annie, not her. "Oh, I have much bigger plans than that for you, Deek." Just for the fun of it, she led him to her bedside, laid her hands on his shoulders, and pushed. It should have made him flop back onto the bed, but it was like shoving a brick wall. "Have a seat, and we'll get started."

She headed for her closet but then stopped and turned around. "I almost forgot. This dress is option one. Does it make me look like I have a food-baby belly?"

"No." He frowned. "It makes you look like you're going to a business meeting."

Leave it to Deek to tell it like it is. "So, not sexy? At all?"

"I didn't say that." Deek hesitated and then cleared his throat. "You look hot in anything you wear. Especially yoga pants, which I sort of miss, by the way. What's option two?"

Lori's cheeks were suddenly on fire. "Be right back." She hurried into her closet and whipped the black sheath dress over her head.

Deek thought she looked good in anything? Even yoga pants? It brought tears to her eyes. She worried she'd lost her figure in the ten years she'd been out of the dating game. He couldn't have said anything nicer to help her confidence.

As she struggled with the zipper on the back of the blue dress, it occurred to her that maybe that was what Deek was doing. Just being nice about her figure. She was a whole lot curvier since the last time she'd been on a date.

She gave up on the zipper that was only three-quarters closed, then slipped into the tall black heels that killed her feet, but she hoped made her legs look shapelier. Her stomach roiled as she stood before Deek again. "Is this one any better?"

A grin lit Deek's face as his gaze traveled up and then back down her entire body. The lust in his eyes made her shiver. And wish she was staying home and eating sandwiches with sexy, geeky, fun Deek instead of going on a first date with Jason.

"That's the winner. Your date is one lucky guy, Lori. You look beautiful."

The sincerity in his gaze made her question if the lust she noticed a moment ago could mean he was changing his mind about their relationship? Being more than just friends? Annie'd said he could date others.

Nope. Silly to think so. He was determined to win her back. "Thanks. Can you help me with the back?"

"Absolutely." He stood and laid his hands on her shoulders before he slowly turned her around. The warmth of his strong hands seeped through the thin layer of fabric.

After he'd moved her long, curly hair aside, he gently tugged on her zipper and whispered, "This side looks great too." When she was all zipped, both his hands slid to her waist, and he gave her a light squeeze. "Very nice."

Her heart skipped a beat at the husky desire in his voice. Her butt was one of her greatest concerns. She did extra squats every day to stave off any more spread. "Thank you, Deek."

He stood behind her with his hands still on her waist. The reflection showed how well their bodies fit together. She was tall, but he was a head taller. And those big hands… She needed to stop. Jason. She needed to focus on Jason.

She turned around and noticed his T-shirt for the first time. It said: *You can't please everyone—you're NOT pizza!* It made her smile. As always. "Nice shirt. But now I'm hungry for pizza. Thanks a lot."

"You're a little overdressed for pizza. Where's what's-his-name taking you?"

"His name is Jason." Lori walked to her dresser to choose earrings. "I'm meeting him at that hot new fusion place everyone is talking about."

Deek grabbed his phone from his back pocket. "His last name too, please. And what's the name of the restaurant?"

"Jason's last name is Pederson, Eliot Ness. And the restaurant is called Chuks. It's American, Polynesian, and Hawaiian cuisine."

"Seafood caught fresh from the oceans surrounding Denver? Makes no sense. And how do you know this guy is safe? Maybe we should have a code word or something in case you need to be rescued. If you'd like, I can put a tracker app on your phone." He started tapping, and then his head whipped up. "That sounded stalker-ish, didn't it? I meant for the evening. For safety… I'll stop talking now."

Deek was so sweet. It made her heart go all gooey.

As she slipped on her favorite dangling earrings, she said, "I'll be fine. Jason filled out one of our applications. My sister-in-law, Shelby, ran a background check on him as we do for all our clients, and my brother, Nick, had one of his cop friends check Jason out too. They're both very protective of me. But I appreciate your concern."

Deek put his phone away. "Sounds like you have a great family."

"I do." She nodded. "But they've been so overly worried about me since Joe died that they can be a bit smothering at times. Like with Emily's tuition. I wanted her to go to the best schools she could, but when I saw the price, I gave up on that idea. She'd be fine in public school; private is a perk we could live without. But the next day, I got a text from the school saying Emily would get a full-ride scholarship because her father was killed in the line of duty."

"That's what the money is for. I donate to the scholarship fund all the time."

"Yeah. But that same morning, I'd mentioned to Shelby that Em couldn't go to private school until I got my degree and a better job. Later, I found out my parents had come to my rescue and asked the school to make it look like a scholarship. I appreciate it, and if it'd been anything else, I would've refused, but it was for Em. I'll figure out a way to pay them back eventually. I plan to fix up and then flip this house and hopefully make a few extra bucks to help. It's a matter of pride, you know?"

"Sure. Except I help my dad because...he's my father. I'd never want to be repaid. When my absentee mother came out of the woodwork and asked, it was a harder choice."

Lori glanced at her watch and sighed. "I'm listening but late. Walk with me. I want to hear what happened." She grabbed her coat and headed down the hallway. "Did you give her money?"

Deek caught up in two long strides and walked with her toward the garage. "I didn't have the heart to say no when she told me it was because her husband had just died. She needed somewhere to live until she got back on her feet. It was probably all a lie, but she's my mother. And I have plenty. So I gave her a one-time-only payout."

Lori stopped and laid a hand on the side of his stubbled face. The woman had abandoned her son, and yet Deek still came through. "I think you are the kindest person I've ever met, Deek." She laid a quick kiss on his cheek. "There's homemade PB&Js for you and the kids. Bye."

"Bye." He stuffed his hands in his pockets. "Are you sure no tracker?"

"I'm sure. I'll be back no later than eleven, Dad." Lori smiled and kept on walking toward the garage.

He called out, "What was that about the PB&Js?"

She glanced over her shoulder. Deek stood in the hall with a puzzled look on his face.

"The homemade part was a joke. About cooking meals for the kids—never mind. I laid everything out, but you're going to have to put the sandwiches together yourself."

His face brightened as a realization hit. "Sarcasm again. Will do. See you later."

Still smiling, Lori opened her car door and slid behind the wheel. Something about being with Deek had chased away all her anxiety. As he usually did. He made the idea of fixing up her house less ominous, and he was a whiz with economics, so she'd aced her last test. Having Deek in her life had just brightened it.

What the hell was wrong with Annie? Deek was a handsome, adorable, caring man. A one-of-a-kind…and not an option for her, unfortunately.

She'd grown up in a broken home too, so she understood why Deek was working so hard to get Annie back. From all the phone calls she'd helped Deek make, it became apparent Annie really didn't have much free time to talk. Maybe she was more interested in Deek and Asher than she appeared to be sometimes in her haste.

Lori headed out for the restaurant, determined to make an effort to enjoy her date, hoping for the best.

After circling the block three times, she found a spot and crammed her oversized SUV into a spot better suited for a Mini Cooper. She checked her hair in the mirror and made sure there wasn't anything in her teeth—unlikely because she hadn't eaten since breakfast due to the food-baby tummy fear—then she worked up the courage to meet her date.

Steeling herself, she opened her car door and shivered at the icy blast of January chill as she hurried for the warmth of the nearby restaurant. She grabbed the big wooden door's handle and stepped inside.

She spotted Jason right away as she entered the crowded little bar and restaurant. He was the best-looking man in the place. He sat at a corner table with two drink glasses. One empty and the other half-full. Had he been searching for some courage too, but in the form of alcohol?

Scents of pineapple, seafood, and, oddly, BBQ sauce tingled her nose as she forced her feet forward and across the room. Pizza was sounding better by the moment.

Jason finally glanced up from his phone long enough to notice she was almost at his table. She forced a smile. "Hi, Jason? I'm Lori." She stuck out her hand.

He halfway stood, his gaze checking her out from head to toe before he gently shook her hand. "Great to meet you, Lori. You're a little late. Have trouble finding the place?"

Did ten minutes constitute being late for a date these days? She'd have to work on that. "No. Just running behind a bit. Have you eaten here before?"

Instead of standing up the rest of the way and pulling out her chair for her the way her husband would have done, Jason sat and watched her slip out of her coat, his eyes assessing every inch of her.

He finally said, "Yes. It's my new favorite. I love the combo of pork sliders and lobster rolls."

"The lobster rolls sound good." She picked up her menu and scanned it. She wasn't a picky eater by any means, but the weird combinations didn't make any sense to her.

Jason leaned closer. "I like your dress. Who designed it?"

Only a man dressed nicer than her would have asked that. By the sparkle of his Rolex and the cut of his suit, it looked as though he valued fine clothes. "I have no idea. I got it on sale at Macy's."

"It's refreshing to meet a woman confident enough to buy off the rack." The corner of his mouth lifted as if he'd been teasing. "In any event, the color goes well with your skin tone."

"Thank you." She'd never given a second thought to her skin tone when picking a dress. Maybe she'd pay more attention in the future.

A young, good-looking waiter appeared and asked if she'd like a drink. Before she could answer, Jason held up his glass and said, "Bring me two more while you're at it."

The waiter nodded politely and then turned back to her. "For you, ma'am?"

"A glass of house white wine is fine. Thanks." She didn't want to order something too expensive and make Jason think she was a jerk.

Jason held up a hand. "No. Don't bring her that crap. Bring her one of these."

"What are you drinking?" she asked.

"Don't worry. You'll love it." He waved the waiter away. "Your profile said you're a foodie like me, right?"

"I do love to eat." Shelby must've snuck that in her profile after reading his application. She'd never say she loved to eat on a dating site.

"Order whatever you'd like and enjoy it to the fullest. That's my plan. And then tomorrow, I'll hit the gym right away." His eyes drifted away again. As if he was bored with her.

"Yeah, I always have good intentions to work out, but then something always comes up that seems more important." Like paint a wall or strip wood floors. But that was exercise too.

He looked at her again. "That's why having a work-out buddy is best. For motivation and to keep you honest. You'd be welcome to join me tomorrow. Gotta keep it lookin' good, right?" Jason beamed the same smile that had looked sexy on his application, but in person, it seemed off. Maybe it was the spray tan in January that made his teeth seem unnaturally white. And his hair had so much product, it didn't move when it should have. No one could argue that he wasn't well groomed, though. It looked like his manicure was way fresher than hers. Even his woodsy-scented aftershave smelled expensive.

"The gym sounds fun, but I have plans with my sister tomorrow." Lori glanced at the menu again, struggling to find something appetizing. And now low calorie and low carb to keep it lookin' good. "So, Jason. What made you decide to pick our matchmaking service?"

He finished off his second drink. "My parents are eager for me to settle down and have kids. I work for my father's business that emphasizes clean, family values. I want to keep the old man happy, so I figured I'd give a real relationship a chance. You have a kid, right?"

"Yes." She nodded absently while desperately searching the ala carte menu for a low-calorie piece of fish. She'd probably add yucky steamed veggies on the side. "Emily. She's seven."

"Seven. That's probably a good age. Still young enough to accept another father figure in her life?" Jason's eyes followed their waiter as he weaved through the tables. Yearning for their drinks maybe?

"I'd never want to replace her memories of her father, but yes, I think she'd be open to sharing me with another man."

"That's good." Jason nodded as he finally turned his attention back to their table to study his menu. "And never having to worry about money again would be great too, am I right?"

"I suppose." She wasn't sure what Jason meant by that, but maybe he was just as nervous as she was. When she looked up again to ask Jason another question, her stomach dropped.

Melanie, former best friend, and the woman who'd slept with her husband stood at the bar. Flirting with a man. Much like she used to flirt with Joe. Lori had been a trusting idiot to think it'd been harmless.

Seeing Melanie again brought back a tsunami of painful feelings. But mostly betrayal. She felt as if she really might be sick if she didn't leave. She couldn't deal with a first date and seeing Mel again for the first time since Joe's funeral. "Jason, I have to apologize. My daughter had been sick last week, and I'm afraid I might have caught her bug. I'm not feeling well, suddenly. May I have a raincheck?"

"Oh. Sure, I understand. I'll walk you out." The relaxing of his shoulders and the relief on Jason's face made her feel even sicker to her stomach. She'd taught clients to read body language cues, and his showed that he clearly wasn't interested in her. Or so nervous he was relieved he wouldn't have to go through the paces?

Dammit. What a nightmare. Maybe Deek *had* just been being nice about her appearance earlier.

She stood. "No. Stay and enjoy your…drinks. I'm good." She slipped into her coat as Jason continued to watch their waiter. "Good night."

Jason finally turned his attention back to her. "I'll be in touch in a few days. I'd like to see you again."

Sure he would. "Sounds good. Take care."

Lori hurried toward the front door. As she weaved through the busy restaurant, a delicate hand landed on her arm.

A familiar voice said, "Lori? Can we talk? Please?"

She sucked in a deep breath and slowly turned to face Mel. "There's really nothing—"

"I've tried texting and e-mailing, but you've obviously got me blocked. For good reason. But if you could find it in your heart, could we please meet for coffee one day? I miss you so much. And I'd like the chance to explain."

The tears burning in Lori's eyes wanted to fall, but she refused to let them. She'd loved and been best friends with Mel since elementary school. Her betrayal was in some ways worse than even Joe's.

As she gazed into a set of remorseful brown eyes, all the love Lori used to have for Mel came rushing back. But how could she ever forgive her? "I don't know… I'll think about it. But I have to go."

Mel blinked back tears and nodded. "Thanks. For at least considering it, Lori. My number and e-mail are the same when you're ready."

"Okay. Bye." Lori pushed on the heavy front door of the restaurant, bracing for the slap of cold air freezing the tears to her cheeks as she hurried toward her car.

After she'd started the car and cranked the heater, she headed for home, destroyed by the lack of interest from Jason and the olive branch Mel tried to hold out to her. Why should she meet with the woman who claimed to be her best friend, who'd flown into the town they'd been stationed in, to betray her with Joe?

But Mel had seemed genuinely upset and sincere.

Her traitorous heart was trying to tell her to hear Mel out, but what could she possibly say to excuse her behavior?

Lori's stomach was either really upset now, or she was famished. She laid the back of her hand on her forehead. No fever, so she was just hungry. And way off-kilter.

She spotted Papa G's restaurant ahead and blamed what she was about to do—eat pointless carbs and cheese she didn't need after all the cookies—on Deek's T-shirt. She'd wanted pizza ever since she'd read it. Or maybe she wanted the man who wore the shirt, but that she *couldn't* have, so pizza it was. Hopefully, hot dough and delicious red sauce would drown out all the hurt she'd endured in the last half hour.

Jason, who wasn't interested in her, and running into Mel, the woman her husband had turned to for something Lori apparently couldn't give him, was just the icing on the crappiest day she'd had in a long time.

Deek was hooked. Who knew the silly animated movies Emily and Asher loved to watch were so good? He enjoyed the adult humor slipped in that went right over their heads. Hopefully, Lori was having enough fun on her date that he'd have an excuse to watch the whole movie. The kids had retreated to Emily's room to play video games, so he looked forward to sitting back and enjoying the show in peace.

The rumble of the garage door made him check the time. Lori had been gone for just under an hour. Things must've not gone so well.

He debated turning the channel rather than having to eat crow when Lori saw him watching the movie without the kids. But the movie was awesome, so he'd take his licks.

Lori appeared a few minutes later, her eyes red and puffy, holding a pizza box in her hands. "Hi. Did you guys eat?"

"The kids ate right after you left. I was just about to grab something. Are you okay?"

She shook her head as she laid the box on the coffee table. "I'm going to change. Be right back." Lori disappeared and then returned a moment later with tears in her eyes. "I need help with my zipper. Please." The defeat in her voice sent a dagger to his heart.

After pausing the movie, he jumped up from the couch. As he slowly tugged the zipper lower, he whispered, "Do I need to go beat up Jason?" He'd do it in a heartbeat for her. He loved the time they'd spent together every day. There wasn't anything he'd rather do than be with Lori. When she smiled at him, he felt like Superman. She made him happy.

She glanced over her shoulder and smiled sadly. "While you have the physique, I'm guessing you've never hit anyone in your life, Deek."

"Untrue. I took boxing in college. I studied hours of film looking for proper techniques and practiced until I had the muscle memory. Came in second in our division."

Her right brow arched. "I'm impressed. Be right back. Help yourself to some pizza."

What had Jason Pederson done to hurt Lori? Digging into Jason's private on-line life might give some clues about what kind of guy he was.

Deek grabbed the laptop he'd brought along and was about to do something that wasn't entirely legal, but the chances of being caught were slim. He'd never go public with what he'd find, so he'd risk it. If there were any dirt to find on Jason, Deek would find it.

As he tapped away, he uncovered a gold mine of what Jason surely thought were private pictures. They told an interesting tale. And the number of women he'd posed with showed he was a major player.

Lori joined him on the couch wearing gray sweats and a pink T-shirt that clung nicely to her curves. She picked up the remote and hit Play, and then grabbed two pieces of pizza. She put one on a napkin for him, then dug into her piece.

He paused his computer search. "What happened?"

She took a big bite and then closed her eyes. "I ran into the woman Joe had an affair with before his last deployment. And my date was more interested in the color of my dress than me."

"Then he's blind. I'll never forget the first time we volunteered in the kids' classroom together. I thought you were the prettiest woman I'd ever met. It was just a bonus that you were always nice, and easy to talk to. And the only single mom who didn't flirt with me at school."

"Really?" Lori looked puzzled. "Thank you. I think you're very attractive and easy to talk to as well. Not to mention handy to have around. Apparently, Jason doesn't think the same things that you do about me."

"It's his loss, not yours." He took a big bite of pizza as he debated telling her what he'd found. The guy was all wrong for Lori. But would she think less of him for hacking?

"It doesn't matter. I don't think I was ready to date again, anyway. Especially a guy so handsome he could model for *GQ*.

You can't trust those types. Joe was very Ken-doll handsome too. I need someone nice, who won't look at me with censure for eating cookies because I couldn't resist."

No way could he let Lori think Jason's lack of interest was because of the way she looked. He picked up the remote and paused the movie. "I think you should see something I found—"

"Besides, I think I mentioned that my sister Rachel is moving back home tomorrow. She'll be living here until she finds her own house. She plans to help me fix up this money pit—like you've been so kind to do, Deek. The house is what I need to focus on now." She took another huge bite of pizza, then mumbled around it, "Men can go suck it."

Did that mean all men? Him too? "Okay. I'll go, but not until after I show— "

Lori grabbed his arm. "No. You're fine. I'm talking about men who are in my dating pool. Not you, Deek."

Should he be offended by that? Annie obviously felt the same. "Annie's obsession with sleeping with other men and her asking me to sleep with other women was already making me wonder if all my sex research had been wrong. But now I'm not dating material?"

"Only for me because you want Annie... Wait. Sex research?" Lori finished off her first piece of pizza and started in on the second.

Lori was off limits for him too, so why not explain? "Before I had sex with Annie because she was my first, I did extensive research on how to please a woman. You know. The study of angles, techniques, and erogenous zones to achieve the most intense orgasms."

Lori choked on her pizza.

He patted her back until she was able to breathe normally again. "Are you okay? Do you need some water?"

"More like a stiff drink." She shook her head and laid her slice down. "Stiff might have been the wrong word. I'm good now. Go on."

"I'm thirsty too. Be right back." He finished off his first slice and then rose and snagged two of the beers Lori had been stocking for him in her fridge, before sitting back down. "Cheers." He tapped his bottle against hers.

"Salute." After she had tapped back, she asked. "So, did your research work?"

He shrugged. "Turns out, Annie hadn't slept with anyone else either, so I was never sure. At least not until she'd left for her dig. She'd insisted we both date and sleep with other people since we'd only ever been with each other. Then we'd know for sure if we wanted to settle down together. By the other women's comments and feedback, it became apparent that my research had been accurate."

"Um...wow. That's...interesting." Lori's forehead wrinkled as if she was distressed again before she took a long pull from her bottle.

But she'd said it was interesting, so he elaborated. "For instance. Did you know that the skin on your lips is the most sensitive part of your body? Therefore, when kissing, it's generally much more gratifying if you angle your heads—it might just be easier to show you. As friends, of course. May I?"

Lori swallowed hard. "You want to show me how to kiss?"

"How to optimize a kiss." She looked confused. It was a simple concept.

"Um. Okay. Why not?" She laid her beer on the coffee table. "It's just science, right?"

"Exactly." He slid closer and laid his hand on her warm, smooth cheek. "To achieve the best results, relaxation is the key..." He tilted her head just right and then did the same to his and laid his lips on hers.

Lori's lips were soft, warm, yielding, and tasted of his two favorite things—pizza and beer. Perfect. But then something unexpected happened. The heat from their simple experiment shot through his body, setting his cells on red alert, all the way to his toes. He hadn't meant to add what he'd learned about tongue maneuvers—that just sort of happened on its own. She seemed to have done similar research because her responses to his stimuli were…perfect.

He'd never had a kiss so invigorating.

He pulled her closer, wanting every part of her body touching every part of his. Her fingers tunneling through his hair made his scalp feel as if it was on fire. Then she softly moaned and crawled into his lap.

Her soft curves snuggled against him made him forget about the friendly part of their experiment altogether. While he took pleasure in her hot kisses, his hands explored her enticing curves. She was soft in all the right places and made his Princess Lori fantasies come to life like an Imax theater experience.

Asher's voice called out, "Dad? Can we go home now?"

Reality hit like a wrecking ball to the head. "Absolutely." Deek stood up so fast, Lori would've toppled if he hadn't caught her and saved her from a pizza box face plant. "Why don't you go get our coats, Ash?"

Dammit. Had he just crossed a line with Lori? He studied her face, but she looked more dazed than anything else. Or was she pondering how to end their friendship?

He'd hate that. She was the first woman he'd ever truly enjoyed just hanging out with. Worse, he'd enjoyed that kiss more than any with Annie. Or any woman.

He'd have to tell Annie that he'd messed up. He hadn't meant to, though. So did it still count?

Had he just ruined his relationship with both women?

6

YOU MIGHT BE ABLE TO FOOL THE WORLD—BUT NEVER YOUR SISTER.

L ori wasn't sure what had just happened between them with that incredible kiss, but Deek's face had turned pale as he waited for Asher to return with their coats.

He laid his hands on her shoulders and stared into her eyes. "I didn't mean for that to get so out of control." His fingers gently rubbed at the knots in her shoulders and neck, still there from her tense evening. "Are you mad at me?"

"No. It was...nice. Did you study massage too? You're very good at it."

He jerked his hands away. "Sorry. I've noticed over these past weeks that you carry your tension in your shoulders and neck. I didn't mean anything by it."

"No worries. What's wrong, Deek?" He was acting like the world was about to end, when all she could focus on was if he'd like to kiss her again.

"Annie's going to dump me when I tell her." He winced.

"Annie still says you should date others, so I doubt she'll dump you."

Deek closed his eyes. "She's said that before, but then when I started dating, she got short and pissy with me. She has a major double standard."

That he was more worried about Annie than the mind-blowing kiss they just shared showed her the attraction was still one-sided. She needed to do the right thing by him. "It was my fault, not yours. I shouldn't have kissed you back. It's just been a while, and I wasn't thinking."

He blinked at her. "I liked that you kissed—"

"Here, Dad." Asher shoved a coat at Deek.

He slipped into his jacket. "I don't want to give you the wrong idea, Lori. About us."

Another rejection. She couldn't take any more in one day. "We're fine. And still friends?"

"Absolutely." Relief made Deek's handsome face relax. "We'd better go."

Lori walked the guys to the front door. "Thanks for baby-sitting. See you on Tuesday for the field trip?"

"I forgot about that." His usual cute grin formed again. "Want me to pick you up? You're on the way."

She should say no, to keep things uncomplicated. But something about Deek centered her and made her feel... happy. It wasn't a crime to want to be with him as friends. "Okay. See you around ten?"

"It's a date." He walked behind Asher to the car but then stopped and turned around. "I shouldn't have said date. Technically, it's just more efficient to save gas—"

"Got it. See you Tuesday, Deek. Bye, Asher."

Asher ran back and gave her a tight hug. "Bye, Princess Lori."

She smiled. A hug was nice after the day she'd had. "Thanks for keeping Em company. We'll see you soon."

Lori released Asher and waited until they were all loaded up. She waved as they pulled away in their fancy new SUV and then shivered from the cold as she closed and locked her front door behind her.

Emily stood in the hall with her arms crossed. "You kissed Mr. Cooper?"

Crap. That was what had taken Asher so long to return with Deek's coat. He'd stopped to tell Em. "Yes. But he was just showing me something. It wasn't a real kiss. But these are." She scooped up Emily and loudly laid kisses all over her cheeks.

"Mom! Stop!"

"If I must." Lori carried an uncontrollably giggling kid to her bedroom. "Let's get you all tucked in. And in the morning, Aunt Rachel will be here to see you."

"Yay! Aunt Rachel."

Lori hovered Em over her bed so she could grab her PJ's. When Lori's cell rang in the den, she laid her daughter on the mattress. "Brush your teeth, and get ready. I'll be right back."

"'Kay. But I declare it national rewind night. So we have to do everything backward." Emily walked on all fours backward to her bathroom down the hall, like a dizzy dog.

Smiling at how goofy Em could be, and thankful for how easy it'd been to distract her, Lori walked backward toward the den to appease Emily's silliness. She flopped backward onto the couch while grabbing another piece of pizza from the coffee table. She answered the phone, expecting it to be her traveling sister. "Hola?" She took a big, decadent, tomato, yeasty, pepperoni-and-mushroom infused bite and moaned with pleasure.

"Hi. It's Jason. Just wanted to be sure you were all right?"

That was nice. She didn't think he'd ever call her again.

Lori quickly swallowed. Then she laid down the pizza, calculating how much time in the gym she'd have to put in to offset the carb and fat content. "I'm feeling much better now. Honestly, I think I was just having first-time-back-in-the-saddle jitters. Thanks for checking in."

"Absolutely. Glad you're okay. And since you're feeling better…" An awkward silence filled the air for a moment until he cleared his throat. "I was wondering if you'd be free to go to a fundraiser with me Monday evening? But before you answer, you need to know that my parents will be there. I'm sure they'll fawn over you in an obnoxious way, being you're so pretty. And nice."

"Thank you." She'd been so sure he wasn't interested in her. Was her radar out of synch after all these years?

She'd have a built-in babysitter with her sister staying. So why not? "What time and where?"

He gave her the details. "Thanks, Lori. You'll be doing me a great favor. See you then."

"I'll look forward to it. Night."

"Good night."

Maybe he'd been as nervous as she'd been at dinner. Was that what she'd been picking up on, instead of ambivalence? That he called showed a lot of compassion, and she liked that in a man.

Shrugging at her miscalculation, she rose from the couch to tuck Emily in. Jason might not be so bad after all. And if she were lucky, he'd kiss as well as Deek.

At home, Deek tucked Asher in, still kicking himself for kissing Lori like that. And for liking it so much. "Night, bud. Sleep tight." He rose and headed for the light switch before he got peppered with any more questions about why he'd kissed Lori like that. It was the "like that" part he wasn't sure how to explain. Pretty hard for Asher not to have noticed that Lori had been in Deek's lap and he'd had both hands filled with her enticing rear end.

Asher called out, "I think Mrs. Went is nice, Dad. And very pretty."

"Yep." He couldn't argue with either of those things. "Good night, Asher."

"Mr. Raymond smiles funny at Mrs. Went the same way you do."

Asher and Emily's teacher liked Lori? "I don't smile funny at Lori. GO. TO. SLEEP. ASHER!"

Deek closed Asher's bedroom door. Just as Deek started for his downstairs study, he heard a small voice say, "YES. YOU. DO!"

He chuckled as he walked toward the steps. He probably did smile funny at Lori. Especially after that hot kiss. He'd better find a way to cover up his affection for her when Annie came home.

Soon. Hopefully.

Guilt crept further into his gut with every step he took toward his study. He shouldn't have kissed Lori like that. Should he come clean with Annie and confess? Or would it cause more problems between them? He hadn't meant for it to happen. That he enjoyed it so much wasn't technically his fault. It was simply the result of an experiment.

Nope.

He was lying to himself. He was as much attracted to Lori as he genuinely liked being with her. Might as well admit it. And be sure nothing like that kiss ever happened again. A grown man could control his hormones. Even the intense ones that had raced through his veins as if he'd still been a horny teenager. He needed to table what he wanted, to be with Lori every day for the rest of his life, and do the right thing. Get Annie home so Asher would have his mother in his life again.

Deek pondered how to go about doing that as he sat down behind his desk and got back to digging into Jason Pederson's background. There had been hints of more hidden data, and he had better snooping equipment at home rather than on his laptop. Top-notch equipment that rivaled mission control in Houston. His incredible electronics were the one area he geeked out the most but had zero guilt about it. He needed it all for his gaming software design. Well, most of it anyway. Now he'd use the most advanced parts for a good cause. Lori.

Grateful he'd been recruited in grad school to help develop profile programs for government agencies, and even more so that he'd quit because it seemed so intrusive, he put those skills to work.

As his machine ran a mining algorithm that automatically dug into Jason's online life, thoughts of kissing Lori again made it hard to concentrate. But then, the results popped up on his screen and drew him right back into his mission. The information intrigued him. Seems Jason had access to sources who charged big money to bury data. But Deek was better and found that Jason had been engaged twice before. Two beautiful, dark-haired, very rich women, but the reasons the engagements abruptly ended were mysteriously never mentioned.

The next set of unearthed photos were so sexually charged and explicit, it was no wonder someone had paid to bury them.

Earlier, Jason had looked like a player on the surface, someone who'd dated dozens of beautiful women in different stages of undress and drunkenness. The sheer number of women made Deek conclude that Jason would tire quickly of a kind woman like Lori; however, the new pictures added a different dimension. Whips, chains, restraints, and men and women engaged in violent orgies filled his screen. A sense of darkness made a shiver run up his spine. The vibe was…vile, not a dress-up party for bored, rich people. Was that a true reflection of Jason's sexual preferences? If so, why would he want a sweet, single mom who wears sexy yoga pants instead of leather?

Unless Lori was secretly into that too?

No. She couldn't be. It was too dark and brutal.

But how would he bring something like that up to be sure? For all he knew, Lori could have a kinky side, and how embarrassing would that be if he called her out on it? And he'd have to admit to his snooping. Either way, he'd need to figure out how to approach the topic before Tuesday when he saw her again because he'd never let anyone take advantage of Lori.

Lori awoke late on Saturday morning with a smile plastered on her face despite the fact that she'd dropped her phone, one she couldn't afford to replace, in her bathtub the evening before. Soaking the tension of the day away while texting with her sister late at night would cost a pretty penny.

But she'd missed her twin sister so much. They hadn't seen each other since their brother, Nick's, wedding the previous summer in Italy. Lori was eager to catch up. Their weekly check-in calls and e-mails were great, but having her sister under the same roof for more than a week hadn't happened since they went their separate ways in college.

After Lori had ordered a replacement phone online, she showered and dressed. The lovely scent of brewing coffee led her to the kitchen where Emily sat, eating a bowl of cereal and playing a game on her phone.

Lori grabbed her favorite blue mug that Em had made from the glass front cabinet. "That uncle Nick bought you a cell phone you're way too young to have is bad enough, but now you're drinking coffee?"

Emily looked up from her phone and grinned. "Aunt Rachel told me to push the button on the machine fifteen minutes ago. She'll be here any minute."

Grateful the coffee was hot and ready; she poured herself some. "What happened to not calling Aunt Rachel because she's driving again today?" She'd been driving to Denver from New York the last three days.

"She called *me* because the Rule Follower would yell at her for talking while driving even though she's using hands-free. She needs coffee the minute she gets here, or she'll die."

"Still so dramatic." Rachel, who Lori called DQ for drama queen, had called Lori the Rule Follower their whole lives. Her sister saw rules in a whole different way than Lori did. No wonder Rachel had quickly moved up and become lead counsel for an international company who needed her to figure out how to get past the foreign red tape. They'd worked her so hard, moved her so often, she had to mainline caffeine to keep up. Well, until last month, when she'd gotten so burnt out, she'd quit.

But Rachel wasn't being totally forthright about quitting and leaving New York. Lori could feel it. She hadn't gotten the whole truth out of her twin yet. But she would.

When Em's phone vibrated with a call, she answered and listened for a moment. "Hang on," she mumbled around the last bite of cereal. "Uncle Nick says he wants your famous ribs and baked beans for Aunt Rachel's welcome-home party tonight. *Please.*"

"Tell him to feel free to pick that up from The Rib Shack on his way over. *Please.*"

She was having her family over for the first time since she and Em had moved in, even though the house was in a state of disrepair. Much better after Deek's help the last few weeks, but it'd be a good contrast for them to see it before and after the transformation. At least that was what she'd told herself to stave off the need to stay up all night and paint.

Emily relayed the message and then pressed the Mute button. "He said those ribs suck. Make him the ribs, and he'll help you with the scary attic next weekend." Emily crumpled her forehead. "But you were already going to make ribs, right? We bought them yesterday."

"Yes. But don't tell him that. It's my duty to make him work for his dinner."

Emily tipped her head to the side. "Why?"

"It's just what brothers and sisters do." Lori took a long pull from her mug. "Tell him we have a deal. But 'sucked' is a bad word in our house, so as punishment, he has to bring dessert."

"I'm going to tell him it has to be chocolate." Emily grinned.

Lori laid a kiss on top of Em's head. "You catch on quick."

A few minutes later, a horn blasted outside, so Lori and Em hurried out the front door. Rachel had her head in the trunk, pulling out suitcases.

"Hi, Aunt Rachel." Emily leaped toward Rachel. Luckily, her sister was quick and dropped her bag before Emily showed up in her arms.

Rachel closed her eyes and held on tight. "I've missed you so much, sweetheart." When tears leaked from the corners of her sister's eyes, it confirmed Lori's suspicions. Tough-ass Rachel had been through something upsetting she wasn't quite ready to discuss.

After Rachel had put Emily down, her sister turned and, without a word, hugged Lori so hard, it nearly cracked a rib. Lori croaked out, "Need some air, here." Lori leaned back and stared into a face most would call identical to hers. Except for the dark rings under Rachel's eyes. "What's wrong, DQ?"

"Nothing." Rachel forced a smile. "Just missed you guys. Help me lug all my stuff inside before we all freeze to death."

Lori peered inside the slick Mercedes that held garment bags and boxes. "This is everything? All you own in the world?"

Rachel picked up two of her matching designer suitcases. "I gave most of my things away before I left. Now I'm traveling light and tight."

Lori picked up a small leather bag and handed it to Emily. Then she hefted the remaining suitcase and quickly caught up. "Tell me you haven't given away all your sexy shoes too? I have a date Monday night, and I was counting on raiding your closet." Lori loved borrowing her sister's designer heels and clothes whenever they were together. Rachel usually ran a little thinner due to her crazy schedule and missing meals, but it looked like her sister was at a healthier weight now.

"Never." Rachel raised a brow. "Mi closet is su closet for the next nine months. I certainly won't be using it."

Nine months?

After Lori had sent Emily back to get more things, she laid a hand on her sister's arm to stop her. "Why won't you need your clothes for nine months?"

Rachel shrugged. "Because that's when my new house is supposed to be complete. In the meantime, I'm going to be working from here, doing freelance work for the rest of the year. No need to dress up."

Relief had Lori throwing her arm around her sister's shoulder as they made their way back to the car. "Only you would buy a brand-new house on-line without seeing it. But thank goodness. I thought you meant you were pregnant."

Rachel winced and broke eye contact. "I see your twin Spidey sense is still intact."

Lori stopped dead in her tracks. "Ohmygod! You're pregnant?"

"Yep. That's why I'm moving in. I need a Lamaze partner. But if you tell Mom and Dad, I'll have to kill you."

They were going to have a newborn in a torn-up house? They needed to step up the renovation schedule big-time. "You can't hide something like that from Mom and Dad. And what about the father?"

Rachel heaved out a long sigh. "I haven't told him yet. He's sort of famous. And hard to get ahold of."

Lori caught up with Rachel, clasped both of her sister's arms, and turned her around. As she stared into her sister's eyes, Lori asked, "How famous?"

"I'm sure even Emily knows who he is. And he's going to want partial custody. I don't know if I want the twins to be subjected to that lifestyle. I have to figure this out. Soon." Rachel hugged Lori again. "You're the only one I know I can trust with this secret. Will you help me?"

"Of course. We'll sort it all out together. But no coffee for you."

"My doctor said I could have one cup a day, Rule Follower."

"Fine. But no more." Twins? Holy crap. Finding the time to help with one baby would be hard enough; now two?

More complications added to her already overwhelming life. But it was her sister. She'd do whatever it took.

7

SEEING DOUBLE CAN LEAD TO BIG TROUBLE.

Lori hated to leave her sister so soon after she'd arrived, but she had a lunch appointment with Shanan to talk about setting her up on real dates. She'd thought about what Lori had said at the science fair and wanted to see what would be involved.

Lori glanced around the warm little pastry shop Shanan had chosen, while her mouth watered. The decadent aroma of coffee, chocolate, and cinnamon filled the air. Shanan lifted a hand and waved Lori over to her table.

"Hi, there. How are you, Shan?" Lori sat at the little table with a blue-and-white-checkered tablecloth across from her friend and hopefully new client.

"Well. That's debatable. I'm happy to see you, as always. And a little sick to my stomach to see you at the same time. No offense."

Shanan always made Lori smile. "I'm just happy to have some girlfriend time, no matter what you decide to do. But what changed your mind about dating nice men?" Lori studied the menu. Maybe she'd just have a mini turkey croissant. She'd save room for the big dinner for her sister's welcome-home party later.

The waiter came by and took their drink orders. After he'd left, Shanan said, "You know what it's like to be cheated on. And please don't take this wrong, but you're quite the hypocrite by going around and spouting about how being happy again is the ultimate payback for a cheating ex when you're not trying to move on either."

Lori's stomach clenched. "I know. But…"

Shanan lifted a hand. "Let me finish. We've been friends for a long time, Lori. And I love you. So I have decided I'll go first and show you that putting my heart out there is the only way to be happy again. I'm tired of the hate and the inability to trust men I'm hauling around after Mike. It's making me bitter and cynical at the ripe old age of thirty-two. I don't want to be that woman anymore."

That brought tears to Lori's eyes. She knew exactly how Shanan felt. "I don't think you're bitter and cynical. I think you're protecting a bruised heart." Lori took a drink of the ice water the waiter had left. "I've always had a knack for knowing instinctively when two people are right for each other, but I think it's been my curse that I can't do that for myself. My grandmother was a matchmaker too, and she insisted it runs in our blood. But she and my mother had the same problem. All of us chose and married cheaters."

Shanan frowned. "You never mentioned that before. I'm sorry."

"It is what it is. But I have the gift of Emily, so I can't say my marriage was all bad. As a matter of fact, until Joe cheated, I was really happy. But for your information, I went on a date last night and have another on Monday."

"Good for you!" Shanan's hand shot out and gave Lori's a squeeze. "I apologize for the hypocrite remark. And now I can watch and see how you do first, so I withdraw my application. How was the date?"

"Horrible. But he asked me out again anyway." Lori told Shanan the whole story about running into Mel and even the kissing-Deek experiment later.

"Wow." A slow grin lit Shanan's face. "You don't even have to tell me how the kiss was. I can see it written all over that blushing face of yours. Has Deek changed his mind about Annie?"

"No. He still wants Annie back. He's made that perfectly clear." Lori held up both hands. "And no matter how much I enjoy Deek's company and would love a repeat of that hot kiss, Asher deserves to live with both of his parents like Deek wants. I refuse to get in the way of that."

"You aren't the one ignoring your kid. If anyone is doing anything to Asher, it's Annie, not you. I wouldn't worry about that at all, but then, I'm not as nice as you."

"Yes, you are." Lori shrugged. "For now, I'm having fun being Deek's friend, and that's enough."

"Uh-huh. Sure." Shanan sipped her water. "So after that kiss, you didn't have a hot dream about him to keep you warm last night, Miss Pure-as-the-driven-snow?"

She'd had the humdinger of all dreams.

"Shut up." Lori lifted the menu and debated having a brownie for lunch.

"I knew it!" Shanan laughed. "Your face lit up like a Christmas tree when you talked about Deek just now. I think you have feelings for him. And I also think you two would make the most adorable couple. I'm going to hope Deek finally figures out that Annie is a lost cause and he needs to move on. With you!"

A pang of sadness shot through Lori's heart. "That all sounds nice, but it's not going to happen. So let's forget all the dating talk. How's your mom doing these days? Is she still thinking of moving to Florida?"

While Lori listened to all the ins and outs of Shanan's life, she couldn't quite shake the sadness that had weaved its way back into her heart at the "most adorable couple" remark. Just wasn't going to ever happen, and that was it.

Deek had left Lori multiple messages on Saturday, but she hadn't called or texted him back. The more he'd dug into Jason's life the night before; the more urgent the need had become to talk to Lori. Jason wasn't the right guy for her.

It was almost five thirty in the evening. Why hadn't she answered him? Was she mad at him for the kiss?

He'd missed not seeing her every day for the first time in almost two weeks. And now he was worried about her.

He started up the stairs to talk to Asher when a drone zipped by his head in their three-story foyer, then crashed into the wall.

"Why are you flying that thing inside?"

His son appeared at the upstairs loft railing, controller in his hands, working hard to suppress a smile. "Because you said it was too cold for me to go outside and to find something to do inside."

He wasn't in the mood to argue semantics. "That's an outside toy. Do you know what Emily's cell phone number is?" Hopefully, Emily could ask her mom to call him.

"Nope." Asher shrugged. "Maybe if you'd let me have a cell phone too, I'd know."

"Anyone who doesn't know better than to fly a drone indoors isn't ready to have a phone. Grab your coat. I need to go talk to Mrs. Went about something."

They slowly inched their car through the falling snow on Lori's street. Apparently, she had company, by the number of cars in front of her house. It reminded him that she said last week that she was having a welcome-home party for her sister. At the time she'd told him that, she'd been bent over on all fours sanding floors. It'd been highly distracting watching the pendant she wore bounce off her breasts with each thrust of her arm. No wonder he'd forgotten about the party.

He parked the car across the street and turned off the engine, not sure what to do. Bother Lori when she had guests, or talk to her later. Maybe she'd been so busy with her party preparations she hadn't had time to look at her phone. Should he wait until he saw her on Tuesday? As long as he warned her about Jason before they had another date, it'd be okay. Maybe he was working himself up over nothing.

He could tell her on Tuesday on the way to their field trip. But if he did that, it'd be the two of them trapped in the car on the way to the kids' school discussing kinky sex. He'd rather poke himself in the eye with a sharp stick.

Asher called out from the back. "Are we going inside? I have to go to the bathroom."

That solved the problem. He could tell Lori he wasn't going to disturb her, but now he had no choice. Thank goodness for Asher and his tiny bladder.

They clomped through the snow to Lori's front porch and rang the bell. After a few moments, the door swung open, and Asher darted inside. "Really gotta go."

Lori blinked at the blur that was his son and then faced him. A slow grin lit her face. "Well, hello. How can I help you?"

"Hey. Sorry to bother you, but I've tried to text and call you all day. I need to talk to you about something important. But I don't want to interrupt your party."

"Oh. Yeah, the phone went for a dip in the tub. Come in out of the cold. It's just my family."

"Thanks. That's a bummer about your phone." He closed the door behind him and hung up his coat amid sounds of laughter coming from the den.

He took her hand and pulled her inside the living room so he could talk to her before Asher got back. "First, I need to ask you some...delicate questions. Bear with me, okay?"

She tilted her head. "Delicate? Can't wait." She whipped off a drop cloth on the couch and sat down. Then she patted the cushion beside her. "Might as well be comfortable while we chat. Have a seat."

He sat beside her, his stomach in knots, dreading the discussion they were about to have. As he drew a deep breath for courage, he asked, "Did you do something new with your hair?" It looked different than it had the day before. Around the bangs or something.

"I did. Thanks for noticing. Now tell me all about our delicate issue."

"Well, first, I need to ask you about...your...sexual preferences."

She smiled. "Like do I like to have sex in elevators or do it doggie style?"

"Not locations or positions, per se." Oh, God. What had he gotten himself into? "More like levels of...adventure?"

She leaned closer and whispered, "I like a little adventure as much as the next girl. What did you have in mind?"

His collar suddenly seemed too tight. It was hard to draw a deep breath. "How do you feel about whips? And restraints?"

"I think used in the right way they could be lots of fun."

Crap. Things weren't going as planned.

He wiped his sweaty palms on his jeans. "So you're into BDSM and...stuff like that?"

"Is that what you like?" She grinned sweetly at him as if he'd just confessed to liking chocolate ice cream, not deviant sex.

He wanted to leave and never utter the word preferences again.

A warm hand landed on his shoulder. "Hi, Deek. I see you met my sister. What are you two whispering about in here?"

He looked up at Lori, back at the woman beside him whose hair was just a bit different from Lori's, then jumped to his feet. "You're twins?"

The sister sitting on the couch laughed. "I'm Rachel. Sorry for messing with you. It was just too hard to resist." She turned her attention to Lori. "Have you been holding out on me? Since when have you been into kinky sex?"

"What?" Lori turned three shades of red. "That's what you guys were talking about?" She turned and faced him with widened eyes.

An older, attractive, dark-haired woman joined them. "It smells like the ribs are done, Lori." She glanced his way. "Hi. I'm Linda, Lori and Rachel's mother. Are you and your son staying for dinner?"

He was still reeling from the embarrassment that he'd just talked to a complete stranger about BDSM. "Well..."

Rachel said, "Of course he is. We have a million things to talk about, don't we, Deek?" Rachel grinned mischievously as she grabbed his arm and tugged. "You should sit beside me."

Panic set in. He needed an exit plan. Immediately.

"Nope." Lori shook her head and clasped his other arm to hold him in place.

Was he going to be the middle of a twin tug-of-war sandwich?

"Quit teasing him, Rachel." Lori stood on her tiptoes and whispered in his ear, "If you *want* to stay, I'll protect you from my meddling family."

"How many more are there?" He wasn't sure what he had just gotten himself into.

Lori took his hand and pulled him toward the kitchen. "My brother, Nick, and my father will try to act all intimidating and ask a million questions, but they're harmless. My sister-in-law, Shelby, knows all about you. But don't get in between her and dessert. She's pregnant. And you already survived meeting my sister and my mom."

He glanced over his shoulder at the two women smiling as they followed behind. He felt like the turkey on Thanksgiving, about to be carved up and served.

But he still needed to talk to Lori, so he'd play along. Besides, the smoky aroma of the ribs baking in the oven made it impossible to say no. "Asher and I would love to stay for dinner."

After dinner, Lori got the kids situated with chocolate cake at the table in the nook and then headed for the dining room to join the adults. She'd asked Deek's permission first, just in case he didn't want Asher to have any sugar. She was trying to respect Deek's strict rules, but lucky for Asher, Deek made another exception and allowed one small piece.

She laid the cake on the table and sat next to Deek again. "Who's ready for dessert?" Lori glanced at Deek, who'd held his own with her family so far, and couldn't help her smile. "You were probably hoping for pie, but I hope cake will do."

Puzzlement wrinkled his face as everyone at the table snickered. She pointed to his T-shirt. It said: *Come to the nerd side. We have Pi.*

"Ah. Good one." Deek grinned back at her. "A small piece, please."

She just loved how good-natured he always was. He had a great sense of humor, as long as it didn't involve sarcasm. "You got it." She cut his piece and then passed the cake plate to her mom.

Her brother, Nick, said to Deek, "I'm unclear about something. Are you dating my sister? Emily told me you've been here almost every day for the past couple of weeks."

Shelby swatted his arm. "Don't start."

Her mother jumped in. "Nick, he has been helping Lori with her house renovations." She turned to Deek. "Ignore him. Just enjoy your dessert."

"No. It's a fair question." Deek laid down his fork. "Lori and I are just friends. Our kids go to the same school. Nothing more."

Except for that mind-blowing kiss they'd shared. He must've already forgotten about it.

A tinge of sadness poked Lori's heart at the straight-forward tone Deek had used. Almost like it'd be silly that they'd ever be together. And he'd be right. He wanted someone else.

Rachel smirked as she cut herself a huge piece of cake. "Lori's never had a guy *friend* before. Certainly not one she smiles at like that. You must be one special man, Deek."

Her pregnant sister with a secret was going to pay for that one. She said to the table, "Didn't we all just miss Rachel? And her...*glowing* personality?"

Rachel stuffed her mouth with cake as her eyes narrowed. She'd gotten the hint to knock it off.

Dad said, "Yes. We're all glad you're back, Rachel. Now, Deek, I understand you design software?"

All eyes at the table focused on poor Deek, who'd just taken a big bite of chocolate goodness. He nodded as he wiped his mouth with his napkin. "Video games, actually."

"Video games?" Her father frowned as he chewed. "So that's your only job?"

"Dad! Stop." Lori wanted to crawl under the table and disappear. Her family was being so protectively obnoxious. "Deek designs the most popular game on the market, and he's the top programmer in his field. He does very well for himself, not that it's any of your business." She glanced at Deek, whose eyebrows disappeared under the shock of hair that had fallen across his forehead. She whispered, "I googled you."

Deek nodded his approval and then cleared his throat. "Since Lori cooked this wonderful meal, I'm on dish duty."

"I'll help you, Deek." Her brother stood and started clearing the table. Something she'd rarely seen Nick do.

Shelby handed Nick her plate. "Be nice, Nick." She tilted her face up for a kiss. "Or that couch might get lonely later."

Lori smiled as she gathered up dishes while her brother kissed his wife like they were alone instead of in her dining room. Shelby was the only woman who'd been able to put Nick in his place, and he loved it. Their whole family adored Shelby for it. She was perfect for him. It made Lori sigh a little as she pushed the swinging door to the kitchen open with her hip.

Would she ever find that kind of love again?

Deek and Asher were almost home before Deek remembered he hadn't told Lori about Jason the freak. He'd gotten so caught up in the great dinner Lori had cooked, all the nosy questions from her well-meaning family, and then the games they'd played afterward. Playing charades with her family had been so much fun, he'd forgotten to pull Lori aside and tell her what he'd found out about her date. He couldn't remember the last time he'd enjoyed an evening that much. "Did you have a fun time tonight, Ash?"

"Yes!" Asher called out from the backseat. "Emily has fun aunts and uncles. And Mrs. Went makes great food. They have a nice family."

"They do." Deek met his son's eyes in the rearview mirror. "And so will we when your mom comes home."

Asher huffed out a breath. "I don't think she's ever coming home."

A pang shot through Deek's heart. Asher deserved a family like Emily's too. "Mom says she is. After the dig is complete. We just don't know exactly when that'll be."

Asher's forehead crumpled, but he didn't respond.

Deek poked the remote for his electronic gate at the end of his drive. While he waited for it to open, he turned around and faced his son. "Your mom misses you, Asher. I'm sure she'll come home as soon as she's able."

Asher crossed his arms. "She didn't even come home for Christmas. I know you just stuck her name on those gifts. I saw them in the closet where you were hiding them."

Crap. How had he found them?

"Your mom asked me to buy those for you. They don't have those kinds of toys where she is." He turned and drove up the long drive to the house, desperately trying to think of something that might soothe his son's hurt feelings. "Why don't we call Mom after school tomorrow and tell her how much we miss her?"

"She only has time to talk to me on Wednesdays, not Mondays."

"That's not true. It's just the best day for her to talk." But Asher wasn't entirely wrong. Annie told him he had to go back to once-a-week calls yesterday. But an exception was in order so she could reassure their son that she missed him.

After they had pulled into the garage, he turned off the engine and got out. Asher appeared by his side, so Deek slipped an arm around his small shoulders as they stepped inside the house. "I know it's hard not to have Mom here with us every day. But we do okay, don't we?"

"Yeah. I guess." Asher shrugged out of Deek's embrace and headed for the stairs. "I'm going to bed. Good night."

"Night, bud." Deek stood at the bottom and watched Asher, with slumped shoulders, slowly trudge to the top. He was still upset. Asher rarely went to bed without being asked to.

The sadness in Asher's body language made Deek mad enough to go to his study and slap the door closed. He needed to talk to Annie. Tell her enough was enough. Asher's birthday was coming up. She'd better get her ass home for that, or... What?

He slumped into his office chair and laid his head back against the soft leather. If he gave her an ultimatum, it'd backfire. He'd tried it once before and had paid for it ever since. He'd been so angry at her. Who'd leave a five-year-old at home to go on a multiyear dig? He'd told her two years ago that if she left for the dig, she had to marry him first, or he'd take Asher, and she'd never see him again. She left the next morning, saying if that was the way he wanted to act, then he'd have to live with it.

She'd known how much it meant to him for Asher to have a mother, and she'd called his bluff. But he'd feared she'd never come back if they weren't married. Hell, she'd only been home once since that day. On Asher's sixth birthday. Happy that she was finally coming home, he'd gone out and bought a new house, hoping to show her how much she meant to him. That he'd become a success, but it didn't mean anything to him without her to share with him. He'd killed himself for years, designing his game in the evenings and on the weekends until it was finally ready to be sold, garnering the highest price ever paid for a video game to date.

But Annie had walked through the front door of his three-million-dollar home, dropped her dusty duffel bag on the marble-floored entry, and declared it to be excessive and stupid to buy a house so fancy. She was happier living in a tent. And what had changed about him that he'd do that? They'd been happy in their crappy little apartment before he'd developed the game, hadn't they?

Her words had sliced through his heart so deep, he'd sworn it'd be the last time he'd ever surprise anyone ever again.

Calmer now, he leaned forward and called up the video conferencing software on his desktop computer. He'd ask Annie to please consider coming home for Asher's birthday. And if she said no, maybe he'd tell her if she came back, then he'd consider giving her the funding she needed to complete her dig.

It was just damn money, after all. Asher's feelings mattered so much more than cash. And he had plenty. But she'd have to agree to come home more than once every two years if he agreed to the funding.

He waited for the connection, but after ten rings, he gave up. It was two hours ahead of where she was in Peru. They'd have to talk about it later.

He closed his eyes and sighed. Being around Lori's incredible family had made him and Asher both realize what they were missing in their lives. So he'd send Annie an e-mail. Hopefully, she'd see it in the morning and call *them* after school tomorrow for a change.

As hard as he tried to be both parents, it was clear that Lori was doing a better job of that than he was.

He pulled up his e-mail and started typing. He laid out some terms for the million dollars she needed, suggested the number of visits home each year, and even threw marriage in as a line item once again. It'd give her something to throw out and feel like he was compromising because she always said no to that. Then he hit Send, shut everything down, and headed for bed.

As he slid under the covers, he smiled at the trick Lori's twin had pulled on him earlier. Their conversation still made him want to hide under a rock, but Rachel had been a good sport about it all.

Lori's sister was just as beautiful as Lori, but it was interesting that she didn't seem quite as attractive to him. That made no sense; they were identical twins. Yes, Rachel had the same smile, but something in Lori's eyes, the way they lit up when she smiled at him, made his chest feel tight.

Especially the way she'd looked at him during the games earlier. He and Lori had taken the kids on their team for charades and had still kicked everyone's butts. They barely had to gesture before the other guessed the clues right. As if they were of the same mind.

They'd made a good team. He'd never forget how it felt when they'd won and Lori had slid her arms around his neck and snuggled her magnificent, curvy body against his to give him an excited hug. He'd wanted to kiss her so badly at that moment.

He was having a hard time forgetting their last kiss. And fantasizing about what it'd be like to make love to her.

But he didn't want to use her or lead her on. He'd never be able to give her what she wanted, a whole family again, because he had to do his duty. Be a good father to Asher and win Annie back.

For Asher, anyway. He had to come first.

Yeah, giving Annie the money for the dig would probably fix everything. It'd allow her to hire a few more people so she could come home more often, and then they could finally be a family.

Well, after she finished her dig in a year or two.

8

SOMETIMES THE COVER OF A BOOK IS BETTER THAN WHAT'S INSIDE.

Lori dug through Rachel's suitcases, using them as a shopping mall, while helping her sister unpack and settle into the guest room. "Hey, Rachel? This dress might work for me tonight. What do you think?"

Her sister had just returned from another trip from the bathroom to deal with her morning sickness and was lying on the bed with her eyes screwed shut. "I think I'll puke again if I open my eyes to look. But I don't get why you're picking out dresses for Jason instead of acting on your feelings for Deek."

Lori laid the lovely red dress down and sat beside her sister. "Because Deek wants Asher's mother. Not me. We're just friends."

Rachel slowly opened just one eye. "The way he looks at you says he wants *you*. Naked. Even Dad noticed last night. He said you both look smitten."

"Smitten?" Lori shook her head as she stood to continue unpacking. She was more than smitten, but she'd keep that to herself. "He's off limits. End of discussion. Maybe a red dress sends the wrong message? I'll be meeting Jason's parents tonight."

Rachel sighed. "You don't fool me for a second, but fine. I get it. You don't want to talk about it. So let's talk about Jason instead. Maybe he can help you end your celibate streak tonight. Two years is a long time to live in the sexless abbey."

"I'm not going to sleep with Jason tonight. It's only our second date. And the first one lasted all of ten minutes." Lori found a satiny deep blue dress and held it up in front of the mirror. It looked expensive, so she checked the tag. If Jason asked her who designed it, she'd have an answer this time. She read the label and gasped. "Holy crap! This must've cost a fortune."

Rachel chuckled. "I used to make a fortune, remember. But back to your nun-like tendencies. If Jason is as good-looking as you say, why not let him be the one to get you back in the saddle again?"

"I'm a mother. I can't just sleep with someone because I'm only getting lucky with something that's battery operated these days."

"Stop. Don't make me laugh. It makes me nauseous." Rachel laid a hand over her mouth as she struggled to hold back her grin.

"I'm glad you think that's so funny. Because, honestly, if I didn't have Emily to think of, I might just be desperate enough to bring Jason home and let him have the honor of reacquainting me to the game."

Lori hung up the gorgeous blue dress and then dug through Rachel's impressive shoe collection. A pair with red soles practically called her name, so she slipped off her tennis shoes and slid her feet into the prettiest black stilettos she'd ever seen. "You think I'm kidding, but Deek kissed me, and I nearly went off like a rocket."

Rachel sat straight up. "You kissed Deek? When?"

Crap! I shouldn't have let that slip.

She could fib, but her sister would know. They had a sixth sense about each other. "Friday night. After my mini date. He said he'd done sex research to please his ex, and could he show me what he'd learned. As friends. I've never been kissed by a friend like that before."

"Sex research?" Rachel's eyes went wide. "If you aren't going to go after a guy who cares what gets a woman's rocks off, then get out of my way. I want Deek."

"Don't even think about it!" Lori whipped around so fast that she nearly tottered off her high heels. "Seriously."

"Look at you." Rachel's right brow popped. "All green around the gills. You're in love with him."

Lori closed her eyes and sighed. "Deek and I have always gravitated toward each other at school events because we just get along so well. But now it feels different. I care for him. A lot. So much that I'll never tell him how I really feel and possibly hurt his relationship with Asher's mother. Deek wants Asher to have a whole family again and is going to great lengths to make that happen."

Her sister flopped back onto the pillows. "So he's hot, knows his way around the female anatomy, is nice, *and* he's noble too? Why couldn't I have found someone like Deek to lose my senses with instead of Marcello—"

"The twins' father?" Lori sat beside her sister on the bed. "Tell me, Rachel. I can't help unless I know the whole story." Lori's mind raced to think of someone famous named Marcello. Then a possibility dawned on her. "Marcello Romano? The actor? And the sexiest man in the entire world according to most polls? That Marcello?"

"Yes." Rachel moaned. "I need to tell him, but I don't want to. Can you imagine what the kids' life would be like having someone that famous as their father?"

Lori blinked. "Maybe pretty wonderful? I mean the guy is loaded, has houses everywhere, right? They could go to top schools and universities. They'd get to travel the world. How is that so bad?"

"You don't understand." Rachel squeezed her eyes shut again. "It's a nightmare to go anywhere with him. People literally pushed me aside to get to him. And his schedule is insane. He's never in one place for more than a few days at a time. We had to use scheduler apps to squeeze out what little time we could together. We dated for over two years, and I probably only spent the whole night with him twenty times."

"I can't believe you never told me about him." That hurt. They had always told each other everything.

"I didn't think it would last. But then one of us would call because we missed the other, and we'd take up right where we'd left off. I kept thinking every time I slept with him it'd be the last. Never anything serious enough to tell you that I had a boyfriend."

"Did you date other guys while you were with Marcello, then?"

"No." Rachel's wet eyes cut to hers. "I didn't have any desire to be with anyone else."

That she'd never mentioned Marcello meant her sister had real feelings for him. "How did we never see you two together in the press if you dated for that long?"

A sad smile spread on Rachel's lips. "He told everyone I was just one of his many lawyers. And we were careful never to touch each other in public."

"Well, clearly there was some touching going on in private. What aren't you telling me? What's the real reason you're so afraid to tell him?"

Tears leaked from the corner of her sister's eyes. "I'm very good friends with one of his real lawyers. When I found out I was pregnant, I asked her what she thought I should do. She's worked with him for years. She intimated that Marcello has paid for more than one abortion, and he still pays some of the women's monthly expenses even though there's no baby. She thinks they're like mistresses he keeps in different cities or something. So I broke up with him."

Lori leaned down and laid a kiss on her sister's temple. "Maybe there's more to those other women's stories than we know. You should tell him. Maybe he'll actually be happy to know he's going to be a father. Has he tried to call you since the breakup?"

Rachel nodded. "Every day. But I don't answer. He'd started calling me at work, so I quit and decided to move home. I was tired of that crazy job and had been thinking about making some big changes anyway. He's stuck on a movie set on the other side of the world for another month. I don't have to worry about him tracking me down until that's over."

Lori's protective radar went off. "What do you mean tracking you down? Like a stalker?"

"No. He's angry with me for breaking up with him out of the blue because of our busy schedules. That's what I'd told him the reason was. He said in his voice mails he's going to hire someone to find me anyway, so I should just call him back."

Lori couldn't decide if that sounded like a man in love or someone dangerous. Unlikely someone that famous would be depraved. "Maybe you should take the call tomorrow. Tell him the truth. You said your due date is in July, but exactly how many weeks along are you?"

"Nine. But the doctor said twins tend to come early, or they often have to take them a little early. I should be prepared for that." Rachel grabbed Lori's hand and squeezed. "After watching you and Mom deal with a cheating mate, I refuse to share him with other women. I can't live with that.

And I won't have our children raised like circus freaks for the paparazzi to harass their whole lives."

She couldn't argue about not sharing him, but that wasn't the biggest problem. Carefree, rule-breaking Rachel didn't fall in love. She was far too independent for that. She probably feared he didn't love her back and therefore avoided the discussion.

Lori whispered, "Tell him you love him. You might be in for a very pleasant surprise. Or he might break your heart, but it looks like you're pretty heartbroken anyway. What's to lose?"

She slowly shook her head. "I don't want to be in love with Marcello. I just am, dammit!"

Lori smiled. "Sometimes our hearts have minds of their own."

"No kidding." Rachel huffed out a breath. "How about we make a deal? I'll tell Marcello I love him if you'll tell Deek how you feel about him."

"No need. I'm not carrying Deek's babies." Lori's situation was entirely different. She'd known from the beginning that Deek was taken. It was just an unhappy occurrence that her heart hadn't gotten the memo. "See you later. I have to get ready for my date. And to show you I'm not a member of a convent, maybe I *will* consider sleeping with Jason."

Her sister snorted. "I'll look forward to a full report when you get home at the sensible hour of ten pm, Mother Superior."

"For your information, the charity ball goes until eleven, smart mouth. Thanks for the clothes." There was no fooling her sister. Rachel knew Lori would never sleep with Jason on only the second date.

As she walked down the hall to her bedroom, a thought occurred to her and made her stop mid-stride. Sleeping with

Jason might actually make all her lovely dreams about being with Deek stop. Then she could finally get a full night's rest for a change. But sleeping with him would take things to the next level, and she still wasn't sure she could ever fully trust a man. She'd put such a solid wall up around her heart that she wasn't sure it'd ever come down all the way.

She needed to get past that fear, but the thought of making another poor decision about a man was daunting at times. But, she'd never get over her fear if she didn't put herself back out there. And it didn't have to be anything serious. She could just sleep with him, with no expectations on either side, so her heart would be safe.

Should she seriously consider it? Shanan did it all the time and claimed it was fun. Could she bust out of her good-girl box and break her own rules? Her husband's early passing always brought home the importance of living each day to its fullest. Maybe if Jason seemed like a nice guy, someone who could turn out to be datable for more than one night, she'd do it!

Deek was so deep into his programming in his study that when his computer beeped with a call Monday evening, it startled him. He blinked at the screen for a moment and then realized it was Annie.

His e-mail had apparently worked. As he pressed the icon to connect, he called out for Asher to join him.

"Hi, Annie. How are you?"

She smiled weakly. "Better after I got your e-mail about the funding. It'd be nice to have a little more help. It's been a long day. How are you?"

"Good. But I miss you."

"I'm sorry, Deek. I know I've stayed away too long."

"Asher will be here in a second, so please don't mention the funding for the dig. We can talk about that later. He's feeling a little neglected by you." And so was Deek, but the call needed to be about Asher first.

"It's just for a few years." Annie sighed. "We're doing great work here."

A few years in a child's life was a major thing, but Annie could never seem to understand that. "He misses his mom. Have you thought about it? Can you make it home for his birthday? He'd love that."

"I'm rearranging the schedule tonight. Don't make him any promises, though. I have to see when exactly I can be away. It might not be on Asher's birthday exactly."

Deek wanted to fist pump at his almost-victory but held back because Asher walked in the room. "Hey, bud. Mom called to talk to you."

Asher's eyes lit up. "She called? Really?" He trotted up and sat in the chair Deek had just vacated. "Hi, Mom! How's the dig going?"

Deek glanced at his empty water glass and took the opportunity to go to the kitchen for a refill. Once he filled his glass, he decided he was hungry. He spotted the basket of apples his housekeeper had left out for Asher, and grabbed one to eat. By the time he got back to the study, Asher was saying goodbye to Annie.

The conversation hadn't been long, but it'd put a smile on Asher's face. It was late in Peru, so he couldn't blame Annie for being brief.

Annie's face disappeared, and Asher spun around in the desk chair. "Dad, could you drive me to Emily's house?"

"It's after eight? Why?"

"I have to get a book from her. I forgot mine at school, and I need it to finish my homework. It's due in the morning."

"We've talked about this, Asher. I'm tired of having to rush around because you don't manage your time well." Deek hated when Asher left things till the last minute because homework was so easy for him. "It's late. And Lori's new cell won't get in until tomorrow. I can't ask permission to drop by. We can't barge in on them two nights in a row."

Asher's face morphed into the innocent puppy look. "I'm sorry, Dad. I forgot the book because I was hurrying to find you after school today in case Mom called."

Probably not true, but the thought of seeing Lori again made the decision an easy one. "Okay. This is the last time, though. Got it?"

"Thanks, Dad."

Deek shut down what he was working on and then grabbed his keys. They really shouldn't just show up at Lori's house so late. "Did you happen to get Emily's cell phone number last night?"

He nodded. "Yeah. I called already and asked if I could borrow her book. She said she'd leave it out front for me. She and her aunt went to the movies."

"On a school night? I'm surprised Lori would let Emily do that."

"Well, um." Asher's eyes darted around the study. "It's supposed to be a secret. You can't tell Mrs. Went. Please, Dad?"

Asher wasn't making any sense. "Why wouldn't Lori know they went to the movies?"

"Because she went on a date." Asher chewed on his bottom lip. "And Emily's aunt sometimes breaks the rules. Mrs. Went doesn't like that."

"Lori is on a date?" Warning bells went off in Deek's head. "With Jason? Come on. Let's go."

As they jogged to the garage, Asher said, "I don't know what his name is. Do you want me to call Emily back?"

"No. I don't know. Let me think. Just hop in." Deek didn't know what they should do. Lori didn't have a cell, so he couldn't call and warn her.

His gut burned with guilt for not mentioning what he'd learned about Jason the last time he'd seen her. And anger at Jason for preying on someone as sweet as Lori. He couldn't let him hurt her.

He tried to figure out how to find Rachel to ask about Lori as he and Asher drove in silence to Lori's house. Asher was probably so quiet because he thought he was in trouble for forgetting his book. "Hey, Ash? Do you happen to know which show they went to?"

His head bobbed up and down in the reflection of the rearview mirror. "It started at six thirty. Em's so lucky. They were going to have popcorn for dinner."

"Movie popcorn is incredibly bad for you."

Asher shrugged. "But it tastes really good."

Deek couldn't argue that point, so he let it drop while he did the math. Maybe Rachel and Emily would be back by the time they got to Emily's house. Rachel would probably know where Jason and Lori went.

When they arrived at Lori's house, there were lights on, giving Deek hope that it wasn't too late. But he didn't feel comfortable showing up unannounced at the front door, especially when Lori wasn't even home. He handed Asher his phone. "Can you call Emily? Make sure they're still awake? I'd like to talk to Rachel about something."

Worry crumpled Asher's brow as he called. After a quick conversation, he hung up and said, "Emily said she'd meet us at the front door. What's wrong, Dad?"

Deek plastered on a smile. "Adult stuff. Nothing for you and Emily to worry about."

"You're acting so weird." Asher led the way to the front door and knocked. When it swung open, Emily waved them inside.

After Emily had handed Asher the book, they both looked up at Deek with questioning expressions.

He said, "Hi. Is your aunt around, Emily?"

Emily exchanged an "I'm going to kill you" glance at Asher. Then she nodded and said, "She's in the kitchen. Asher, can you come help me with a homework problem?"

Poor Asher. He was probably about to get a dressing down from Emily for spilling the beans about the movie.

Deek poked the swinging door open and found Rachel, arm deep into the cookie jar. "Busted!"

Rachel had screeched before her hand flew into the air, sending three cookies flying. "Geez, Deek. You scared the hell out of me." She bent down to clean up the crumbs. "What are you doing here so late?"

He squatted down to help. "I need to find Lori and warn her about Jason."

She stopped her cleaning as concern filled her expression. "Warn her about what?"

"Sleeping with him. That's what I started to tell her, well, I guess it was you, last night. He's a sick perv. A sexual deviant."

Rachel's hand flew to her chest. "But Lori said they ran a background check on him." Rachel left the cookie crumbs where they were and headed toward the swinging door.

Deek followed. "Background checks aren't as comprehensive as people think. And he's paid someone a lot of money to cover up his online past."

Rachel jogged into the den. "She's at some country club. She left the name and number, in case we needed her." She lunged for the coffee table and grabbed a piece of paper. Then she handed it to him. "How do you know all this about Jason?"

"I was recruited in college to work for the government. For law enforcement. I hope Lori won't be mad that I dug into his past illegally."

Rachel raised a brow. "While my sister is very big on rules, I think she'll see you did this because you care for her. A lot. Am I right?"

He nodded. But his face was getting hot, so he studied the paper. "Do you think I should page her? Or would it be better if you did?"

"Luckily, this fundraiser is supposed to last until eleven, so I don't think we're in danger of her going home with him— yet." Rachel took his arm and pulled. "I think you should go down there and talk to her in person. Go right up to her table, tell her how much you love her, and that you can't bear the thought of her with another man. Then grab her hand and tell her you've changed your mind and that you *will* marry her. Then in the car, you can tell her the truth about Jason."

He pulled up short. "What? I never said I love—"

"I know you didn't say that, Deek. Keep up here." Rachel laid her hands on his shoulders and leaned close. "While I'm sure Lori *wishes* you loved her, you need to put the show on for Jason's sake. They just started dating. He'll figure Lori's taken and move on, am I right?"

He was still processing the Lori-wished-he-loved-her remark. Was that true? Would she be interested in him that way? He thought she only saw him as a friend.

"Deek?" Rachel snapped her fingers in front of his face. "Where'd you go off to? Am I right here? Wouldn't most guys move on rather than get in the middle of the drama?"

Forcing his brain to focus, he nodded. "Yeah, I suppose so. But making a scene could get messy."

Rachel started tugging again. "It'd be better to do it in person. Then Lori won't have to lie and come up with fake reasons to break up with him. Lori hates lies. You'll be doing my sister a big favor."

When they arrived at the foyer, he shoved his hands into his front pockets as he considered Rachel's plan. He didn't want to make Lori lie. But something about it still didn't make sense. "Are you sure a simple phone call wouldn't be quicker and easier?"

Rachel shook her head and opened the front door. Before she shoved him out, she said, "You need to hurry, Deek. She was contemplating sleeping with him because she hasn't been with anyone in years—since her husband died. I'll watch Asher. Go save her from her sex-starved self!"

He raised a finger to make a point about the expediency of using the phone when the front door slammed in his face. Looked like he was going to make a scene.

And save Lori from her sex-starved self.

9

THERE ARE MANY BENEFITS TO HAVING FRIENDS.

Lori gazed over Jason's shoulder at the other couples as he held her close on the dance floor. He was just the right height, about a half head taller than her. Even with wearing her lovely borrowed heels.

She was dancing with the most handsome man in the room. His muscles rippled nicely under his tightly cut suit that highlighted his narrow waist and broad shoulders. She hadn't missed other women sneaking coy glances at him all evening even while he'd held her hand or laid his on her thigh during the auction. A signal to others that he was with her, which she'd liked. The bad part was that it'd made her wonder what those big, strong hands would feel like roaming all over her body.

Despite the barracudas in the room, they'd had a marvelous evening, complete with a wonderful meal and some interesting conversation. His parents were very pleasant, but there was a look in Jason's eyes when he'd glanced her way sometimes that she couldn't quite put a finger on.

He'd smiled at her for picking up the right salad fork, and nodded in approval when she'd waited for him to choose their wine. Or so it'd seemed. He could've just been smiling and keeping her engaged, but it didn't feel like that. It was almost as if she were on display for his parents. Like it was a test to see if she were good enough for them.

He whispered, "Have I told you how beautiful you are in that dress tonight, Lori?"

He had. Three times. It made her wonder if he'd had a bit too much to drink. She'd lost track after he outpaced her early on. "Yes, thank you. And you look very handsome tonight."

"Thank you." His hand on the bare part of her back slid lower, and he pulled her closer. "Your beautiful ivory skin contrasts so nicely with your dark hair. And your long neck drives me crazy. I've been dying to taste you all night. Right here." He gently nipped the base of her neck.

Her engines were already idling fast and ready to go, but that little nip got them revving on full.

Then he lifted his head and smiled at her as he pulled her even closer. So close his crotch snuggled against her belly. Leaving no doubt about how much he wanted her. It sent a shiver up her spine. It had been so long since she'd been plastered against a hard body. And God, how she missed being wanted by a man.

His lips moved to her ear, and he whispered, "Was that shiver for me? Or are you cold?"

He'd felt that? Dammit. She didn't want to seem so needy. "Just a draft. I'm fine."

He took their entwined hands and placed them between them, against her chest. "You are so much more than fine, Lori." When he traced the backs of his fingers over the exposed swell of her breasts, she let out an involuntary whimper she wished she could take back.

The gleam in his eyes turned hungry. "You in this dress should be illegal. It's making me want to do very naughty things to you."

Yeah. She knew just how he felt. "Maybe we should go sit down then. Your parents are probably wondering where we went."

His fingertip slowly slipped lower, while the back of his hand pressed harder into her breast. When he lightly grazed over her nipple, her spine straightened, pressing her harder against him.

He said, "Forget them. Tell me how much you need me, inside of you, pleasuring you until you beg me never to stop. That's what you want, isn't it, Lori?"

Her bad-girl side was nodding her head enthusiastically, while the good girl inside was blowing a whistle and calling foul. "Jason, I don't think—"

"Don't think. There's an empty office just down the hall."

What was she going to do? She needed to make a decision, quick. Her body was screaming for release, and here was a handsome man, ready, willing, and clearly able to satisfy her needs.

It took all her strength to look up at him and shake her head. "I really shouldn't."

He took her arm and started for the door. "Give me one more chance to change your mind once we're behind closed doors."

She tried to dig her heels in, but he was too strong. "No, Jason. Really." But he continued to tug her toward the door. When he tripped on someone's foot, it proved he'd had too much to drink. Because of that, she'd give him one more chance before she resorted to kneeing him in the balls. "Jason, stop. Now."

He abruptly stopped and faced her, but hadn't let go of her arm. "What?"

"I'd like to go back and sit down."

He leaned close and whispered, "You don't mean that." His eyes left hers and landed on her chest.

Oh, yes she did. And he'd better start respecting her wishes.

She was just about to slip a finger under his chin to make him look into her eyes when over Jason's shoulder, the doors parted, and Deek walked inside, his eyes searching the room.

When their gazes met, he smiled at her, and suddenly, all her anger ebbed. He was wearing his glasses, and they made her heart do a little flip. He looked adorable in them.

Deek jogged over and joined them. "Hi, Lori. Is there a problem here?" His gaze dropped to Jason's hand on her arm.

Jason plastered on a fake grin and released her. "No. No problem. We were just going to have some fun." He hitched his brows. "If you get my drift, pal?"

Lori quickly stood beside Deek. "No, we weren't. Will you drive me home, Deek?"

Jason lifted his hands. "Wait. There's no need for that, Lori. I'm sorry. I'll take you home."

Deek slipped an arm around her shoulder. "Nope. She belongs to me." He turned and smiled at her. "I was an idiot, Lori. I'd love to marry you if you'll still have me." Then he laid his soft lips on hers, and he kissed her.

Deek had a way of pulling her under his spell so fast that it made her dizzy. Before she could wrap her hand around the back of his neck and deepen the kiss, he ended it.

He stared into her eyes expectantly, as if waiting for her to say something. When her brain finally cleared from its happy haze, she realized he hadn't meant what he'd just said; he was just saving her. "Well, it's about time you figured that out,

Deek." Then she turned to Jason. "Looks like I'm going home with him. Forever. Have a nice life, Jason."

Jason's face clouded with fury. "You're nothing but a damn tease, Lori. You could have been the perfect woman to satisfy my extremely wealthy parents. You don't know what you're throwing away, bitch." Then he turned and stalked away as curious onlookers began to whisper among themselves.

There was no need for name-calling. Geez.

She drew in a deep settling breath as a somber thought occurred. "I have to go back over there and get my purse."

Deek gave her shoulder a squeeze. "I'll get it. Wait right over there for me." He pointed to an empty table in the rear.

She slumped in a chair and waited for Deek, her mind tossing around the "perfect wife to satisfy my parents" statement. Seemed any woman would do for him as long as Mommy and Daddy approved. She needed to talk to Shelby in the morning and suggest giving Jason his deposit back. His motives for finding a partner didn't appear to have anything to do with falling in love. And he was way too aggressive after she'd told him no.

Deek soon reappeared, weaving through the tables. He stood out like a cactus in the Arctic tundra. He moved about people dressed in formal apparel, while he wore his typical garb of tennis shoes and jeans. His T-shirt said: *If life gives you melons—you may be dyslexic.*

Melons. Lemons.

It made her smile.

Deek held out her purse. "What's so funny?"

"Nothing." She shook her head and stood. Then she kissed him on the cheek. "Thank you. But what are you doing here? Is everything okay?"

"It is now. I'll explain it all on the way home. You look fantastic, by the way."

Lori weaved her hand through the crook of his arm as they walked toward the coat check. "You look pretty great, yourself."

Looked like it was back to square one in the dating game.

Deek glanced at Lori as he pulled out of the country club's parking lot. "I'm sorry about that, but Jason isn't the man he appears to be."

Lori turned and faced him. "In what way?"

He pushed up his glasses, suddenly remembering he had them on. Dammit. He never went anywhere with them, and he especially didn't want them tonight. Not when he was going to ask her something so important. But back to Jason first. "After you came home upset on Friday night, I did a deep dig into Jason's online past. As you probably know, on the surface he looks perfect. But underneath, there's a ton of dirt. Bad stuff."

Lori's eyes went wide. "How do you know this?"

Dammit. He didn't want to upset her any further, but he wouldn't lie to her. Ever. "I crossed some legal lines based on some of my former tech training. What I tell you can't go any further than you and me. You can't even tell Shelby. Okay?"

Lori chewed her bottom lip for a moment as she considered. "Okay. Spill."

She didn't seem angry at him. Yet. "Based on some deleted online e-mail conversations, those never go away, by the way, the right equipment can find anything, it seems he's been engaged two times before. And the women were paid off to keep their mouths shut about his dark sexual appetites."

"What do you mean by dark sexual appetites?"

"Weaponry, pain, bleeding, bondage, dominance… That kind of dark stuff. And the women had both started to plan the weddings before he slipped and let them see his true nature. His parents know about him and have told him he'd be cut off if he doesn't stop. But I wonder if he can."

"Oh my God." Lori blinked at him. "Is that why you and Rachel were talking about BDSM last night? Were you trying to warn me then?"

"Yes. I'm sorry I didn't get the chance to talk to you alone after that."

"That might explain his aggression on the dance floor. The guy wouldn't take no for an answer, and that's never okay." Lori slowly shook her head. "But we did a background check. And my brother checked police records. This isn't good for my business. We need to find a way to access the data that you did."

He cringed. "You can't legally do what I did unless you're actually in law enforcement and have a valid reason. But I'll look into how you can be more thorough and get back to you."

"Thanks." Lori's jaw clenched as she stared out the windshield.

Dammit. She was mad at him. "Normally, I'd never do that. I respect rules. But I hated seeing you come home so upset the other night. I just had to be sure. For both you and Emily. Can you imagine if he'd fooled you long enough to actually marry him? He comes off as Mr. Perfect, right?"

Lori finally met his gaze. "On the outside, yes. In looks only. The bad stuff notwithstanding, he's not the kind of guy I'd ever end up with. I was just…"

He held up a hand. "I know. Your sister told me. You haven't had sex in a long time, and you just needed a release."

Lori's jaw fell open and an "Ach," sound came out. Then she dropped her head into her hands. "I am going to kill Rachel."

Then she moaned.

Like she was in tremendous agony.

Why would she do that? What would elicit moaning when not really in physical pain?

Lori finally sat back up, stared out her side window, and shook her head. That went on for a solid minute.

He needed to fix something, but he wasn't sure what. "Did I say something wrong?"

"No." She blew out a long breath. "I'm just mortified. And feeling a little stupid for even considering sleeping with Jason. But for the record, Mr. Blunt, I told him I wasn't going to sleep with him before you got there."

Mr. Blunt?

Lori must be really mad. What should his next step be? Maybe best to go with honesty. "I was thinking about your problem on the drive to the country club earlier."

"My problem?" Lori slowly turned her head and narrowed her eyes, sort of like an angry cobra might do right before it was about to strike. "Exactly what would *my problem* be, Deek?"

Yep. Angry cobra was about right. "Well, Rachel said you hadn't had sex in a few years, and I was supposed to go save you from your sex-starved self."

"So this night can get worse?" Lori threw up her hands. "Who knew?"

"I thought since we both haven't had sex for a while, it might be good for us, physically speaking, of course, and since Annie said I could, if maybe you and I should sleep together? Just as friends. I have to marry Annie, if she says yes. But I think it'd be better if you had pointless sex with me rather than some guy like Jason. Not that I can't be a little adventer—"

"Stop. Please, Deek." Lori dropped her head into her hands and did the moaning thing again. But the moan was a little different this time. Not so much in pain but more a whimper.

He didn't see the problem. It was a logical solution that they'd both enjoy the hell out of. Why would she be willing to sleep with Jason just for sex and not him? It made no sense.

And then there was the other thing. "Your sister said something else."

Lori let out another long moan. He took that as a sign to go on.

"Rachel said that you probably wished that I loved you. Is that true? Because I didn't think a woman like you would ever be interested in a guy like me." When Lori didn't answer, he added, "You can just moan once for yes and twice for no, if you'd like."

Lori slowly sat up and sighed.

Still looking straight ahead, she whispered, "I think Annie is the luckiest person in the world to have you, Deek."

That didn't answer the question. "Does that mean you like me too?"

"Too?" She finally looked at him. "Do you have feelings for me, Deek?"

He pulled into her driveway and threw the gearshift into Park. Then he turned to her and took her hand. "I have so many confusing feelings about you that I don't know what to do with them sometimes. I love being with you more than any other woman I know. But I have an obligation to Annie and Asher that has to come before how I feel."

She nodded and pulled her hand free. "I know they have to come first. Let's just be friends and forget this whole entire night ever happened. Literally. Okay?"

He wanted her to say she had feelings for him too. But apparently, she didn't. Not like that anyway. "Okay. If that's what you want."

"It is. Night, Deek." She opened her door and got out.

He felt like he'd been stabbed in the heart with one of the icicles that hung from Lori's garage.

As she walked in front of the hood, he rolled his window down and called out, "Wait. I screwed that up." He shut down the engine and got out of the car. "What I should've said was that I wanted to be the first man you slept with since your husband. Because I care about you, and I want it to be with someone who understands that it might be hard for you to be with someone else. I mean… It was for me. After Annie left us." He lifted his palms, begging for better words to express what his heart was trying to say, but there were no more in the well. He let his hands fall to his sides again. "I wanted it to be nice for you, Lori. That's all."

He stared at her, waiting for a response. But she just stood there with a major frown on her face. He'd screwed that up too, dammit. He'd be better off leaving before he made things any worse. "Good night, Lori."

He started back for the car, but before he could open the door, she called out, "Maybe you'd better come inside."

His heart soared as he turned to face her. "Really?"

She nodded. "I assume Asher is here. Probably sound asleep by now."

His heart sank to his tennis shoes. "Right. Of course. I can't believe I almost forgot my son."

He walked beside her to the front door, feeling like he'd lost his best friend. After Lori had punched in the code to release the lock, she opened the door, then shut it behind them. The house was dark and silent. Everyone must be asleep.

Without turning on any lights, she shrugged out of her coat, and then turned and started unbuttoning his.

"Am I staying?" he whispered.

"Yes, please. I'd very much like you to be my first since Joe too." Lori leaned on her tip toes and kissed him. "But you can't stay all night. I don't want the kids to know. And we're just doing this as friends, to end our celibate streaks, nothing more."

"Deal." His heart nearly burst out of his chest as she took his hand and led him toward her bedroom. He'd dreamed of making love to Lori for so long that it'd be hard to take his time, but he would.

He'd use everything he learned to make it the best sex she'd ever had.

10

DOING RESEARCH CAN REALLY PAY OFF IN THE END.

Lori dragged Deek inside her darkened bedroom and then quietly closed the door behind them. She was going to end her celibate streak and sleep with him. Her heart pounded with anticipation. She'd been mortified that Rachel had told Deek the personal things she had, but when Deek said he'd just wanted the first time to be nice, her heart had melted a little.

As soon as the door closed, Deek took right over and pressed her back against the wood. He hadn't had sex in a while either, so he probably wanted it as hard and quick as she did.

He laid his mouth on hers and kissed her until she didn't have a working brain cell left as he quickly tugged down her zipper. When her dress pooled at her feet, she stepped out of it and then stopped kissing him just long enough to lift his T-shirt over his head. There was enough moonlight to cast sexy shadows on all the hard planes of his sculptured chest. The man must work out every day. Her fingers traced along each bump of his six-pack abs as she continued their kiss.

He opened the clasp on her pushup bra, removing it in record time, in their race to get each other naked. When she reached for the zipper on his jeans, his hand covered hers. He lifted his mouth just enough to whisper, "Not yet. It's all about you first." His large hands cupped both her bared breasts and gave a gentle squeeze. "Besides, I want to take my time exploring. I just love your body, Lori."

His mouth joined in with his hands pleasuring her chest and making her knees grow weak, so she held on to his broad shoulders, closed her eyes, and enjoyed. Lost herself in the sensations pulsing through her body with each stroke of his tongue across her needy breasts. Her head dropped back against the door with a thunk as she let herself drown in the sweet pleasure he gave her.

Her hands explored all the hard ridges on his upper back and shoulders while he slowly slipped her panties aside and slid a fingertip right where she ached most for him to touch.

He whispered, "Just let go, Lori."

She shook her head. She wanted to wait for him to join her. "I can—"

Then he plunged two fingers inside her, slowly stroking her until she considered changing her mind about waiting for him. "Maybe I—" Her back arched, and she moaned as a wave of pent-up need overcame her, made her body throb around his fingers, matching his rhythm with her hips as he moved in and out of her in long steady strokes. His thumb still teasing her, circling and pressing at the same time drove her insane with need. It was like no experience her battery-operated lover had ever given her. Like no experience any man had ever given her, and it pushed her straight to the edge. She had no choice; she couldn't wait. "Deek, I—" Before she could finish her sentence, the dam filled with years of unbridled lust broke, and she came so hard, and with such breath-stealing relief she hadn't had in so long, it made her want to weep with joy.

She laid her head on his shoulder while she caught her breath. "Thank you for the research, Deek. So far, it's spot-on."

"Your sexy moans were worth it alone. But there's so much more I want to show you." He kissed her again while maneuvering her toward the bed. She couldn't wait for round two. Or maybe ten, if he was up for it. She certainly was.

When they got to the edge of the bed, he sat down and drew her between his legs, and then he slipped her panties lower. "Let's get these out of the way, but if you don't mind, I'd like you to keep the heels. You look incredibly sexy in just them." He leaned back on his hands and studied her with a hungry smile on his face. "And now that we got the first orgasm out of the way, I want to look at you."

Good thing it was just dark enough that Deek wouldn't see all her flaws, or she'd never be brave enough to stand before a man in only a pair of heels. No amount of exercise could erase all the effects of once being pregnant. "I was just thinking that I'd like to see you in nothing but your glasses. Show's over, buddy. Your turn to get naked."

"Pushy in the bedroom. I like that." Deek smiled and slipped his hands around her bottom, pulling her closer. Then he reached down and unzipped his jeans to give himself more room. He'd been practically busting out of them. "Maybe I should explore with my mouth instead of my eyes for a bit."

She nearly whimpered. She already knew what his fingers could do; she couldn't wait to see what he had in store for her next. He reached up and kneaded her breasts again, moaning when her nipples grew hard under his expert caresses. Then he grabbed her butt and drew her body against his mouth. "It's all about pressure and angles. And sensitizing the nerves." His mouth was moving lower, toward her already throbbing center as he crossed her not-as-flat-as-it-used-to-be belly, slowly laying soft kisses on her skin, tracing circles with his tongue, and building huge anticipation for when he found his target.

He parted her with his fingers, ran circles around her sensitive skin before his tongue joined the party, sending a jolt of sensations through her body again. Between the patterns his fingers made, and the sweep of his tongue, she didn't know if she could stand any more stimulation. "Deek. I need—" She fisted her fingers in his thick hair and pulled him closer. She didn't know if she wanted him to stop, or if she'd kill him if he did.

He seemed to know just when to press harder and when to go a little slower, keeping her just on the edge of insanity. She needed to lie down before her legs gave out.

As if he read her mind, and without stopping, thank God, Deek lifted her up as if she weighed nothing, and laid her on her back as he kept up the good work between her legs.

She needed release again and writhed under him with every new stroke. Reaching above her head, she hung on to the posts in the headboard to keep her grounded as her hips jerked involuntarily with his sweet torture. "Deek. Please. Now."

She opened her eyes and found that Deek had managed to kick out of his jeans and was fumbling with a condom, all while he pleasured her. He was an amazing lover.

He finally stopped long enough to roll the condom on his very impressive erection, and then he slid his hands slowly up her body, as he slipped all the way inside her. He was large, but she was so ready, it didn't matter.

Deek covered her hands with his on the headboard posts and whispered, "This is just how I dreamed of you. Beautiful, naked, back arched, hands above your head, begging me to take you."

She nodded while her body thrummed inside, yearning for him to do just that. "Me too. Hurry. Please."

He thrust into her so hard that she couldn't help her out-cry. Then he did it again, and again, and she never wanted him to stop. Her hands trapped under his wanted to touch Deek, to explore his hard chest above her, his strong thighs, his muscled ass that kept up the steady plunges inside her, but he held her in place, and with each new thrust pushed her to another level she'd never gone to before. It stole her breath, made her muscles weak like she'd just float right off the bed if he hadn't been holding her in place. So she closed her eyes and rode the wave that had built into a fierce storm inside her and let herself bask in the pleasure Deek gave her.

He lowered his mouth to hers and kissed her, so deeply it stole the last of her strength, and she needed to give in, enjoy the quivers up her spine as her body tightened around his. It had to be torturous for Deek to hold off so long. So she whispered, "Together," and then she came with an intensity she'd never known before, while he found his much-needed release at the same time.

He finally moved his hands and slowly lowered his heavy body on top of hers as he gulped for air. Then he buried his head on the pillow beside her and kissed her cheek. "You okay?"

"Mmmmmm," was all she could manage as she lay under him, waiting for the aftershocks of the incredible sex they'd shared to completely still.

Deek must've felt them too, because he whispered, "I think we're going to have to go another time. Can't leave my princess wanting more."

She smiled and ran her hands over his damp back. While caressing the sexy, hard cords of muscles that heaved along with his attempts to gain his breath back, she whispered, "But I want to be in charge this time."

"Still being bossy?" He lifted his head and kissed her, slowly and sweetly. When his lips left hers, he whispered, "I haven't shown you everything I've learned yet." He stood and headed to the bathroom.

"Seriously?" She propped her head up on one hand. "There's more?"

He called out, "Uh-huh. But if you want to have it your way, I'm game." After a few minutes, he returned, obviously without an ounce of modesty for being completely naked, and slipped under the covers again. He pulled her beside him, his hardness against her leg proving the next round was imminent. "So what'd ya have in mind, Lori?"

She loved how confident he was in the bedroom. It was a major turn-on.

"Well, even though I'm a princess, and used to bossing people around…" She slipped his thick black glasses from his nose and laid them on the nightstand. "I can be a fair sovereign too." She snuggled next to him again. "Feel free to proceed."

"Your wish is my command. Get ready to lose all control." He flipped her onto her stomach, then lifted up her hips to the angel he wanted. "Probably best to rest on your elbows for this."

As she knelt before him on all fours, feeling more foreign but incredible sensations, she didn't know how much more she could take of his glorious torture to her body, but she'd gladly die trying.

Deek blinked his eyes open, unsure of where he was for a moment. Then the warm, curvy, naked woman wrapped up in his arms moved, proving it hadn't been all a dream. But he wasn't supposed to be there. "Crap. I fell asleep."

Lori's head popped up. "You have to sneak out. And then come back with clothes for Asher, so the kids won't know you spent the night."

He glanced at the clock on her nightstand. "Too late for that. What else you got?"

Lori sat up and held the sheet against her chest. Seemed a little late for modesty after what they'd done for most of the night. It made him smile. "Hey. In case I forgot to tell you, last night was awesome."

When she turned to look at him, the annoyance at their situation slowly slipped away, and she smiled. "It was." She laid a hand on his cheek. "Thank you for all the studying on how to please women."

"I added in a few special things just for you." He leaned over and kissed her. He loved kissing her. And she was incredible in bed—in a really noisy, sexy way.

He'd enjoyed hearing and watching how much pleasure he'd given her. But she could've written some of the books he'd studied. When he'd finally let her please him, she'd had him begging for more. He hoped they could make love again. Soon.

She slowly ended the kiss. "I really liked those special touches. Now get dressed and then grab a pillow. Let the kids find you on the couch when they get up. We'll just say it was late and the roads had iced over."

"That's probably true, so it works for me." He jumped out of bed and gathered his clothes scattered about the room. Lori leaned back against the headboard and watched. Like a hungry lioness waiting to pounce.

He wished she'd get her naked ass out of bed so he could watch her dress too, but she was probably waiting for him to leave. He never knew what to do with morning afters.

He crossed to the bathroom and found Lori's robe on the back of the door. So he grabbed it and then sat beside her on the bed. "Here's this, but I couldn't find your crown, Your Majesty."

"I keep it locked away in my castle. Along with all my designer shoes." She smiled as she slipped into the robe, managing to show very little skin, unfortunately.

He picked up one of her sexy heels off the floor so she wouldn't impale her bare feet when she got out of bed and noted the red bottom. He quickly shut down the memory of her standing before him wearing nothing but those shoes. He had to get to the couch before the kids woke up, not ravish Lori one more time. "I thought you said you didn't have any of these."

"Those are my sister's shoes." Lori plucked his glasses off the nightstand and slipped them onto his face. "How am I going to be able to look at you today during the field trip knowing what we did last night?" She slid out of bed and headed for the bathroom. "Don't take it personally if I ignore you. I think the kids will figure it out otherwise."

He caught up with her and wrapped his arms around her waist to stop her. "Is it that, or are you afraid of making Mr. Raymond jealous? Asher says he smiles at you funny."

She turned and hugged him. "Does he? I never noticed." Then she kissed him. "But I bet he hasn't done his research like you have. I'm worried you've spoiled me for all other men, Deek. Seriously. I've never…"

His heart soared. Maybe last night hadn't been a one-shot deal after all. "Never what?"

She leaned her mouth next to his ear and whispered something so erotic that it made him rock-hard. Then she said, "You'd better hurry to the den."

"Way to leave a guy hanging." He gave her butt a playful pat and then grabbed a pillow and a blanket from the bed. "I'll start breakfast once the kids are up. Take your time in the shower. Unless you need a hand?"

"Don't tempt me." Lori grabbed him by the shoulders, turned him around, and pushed him toward the door. "Get out before I cave again to your woo-woo spells or whatever they are."

"The scientific term is Kama Sutra."

She whispered, "Well, kindly take the sutra and all that karma of yours to the den."

"No, it's—"

Lori held up a hand. "I know. It was a joke, Deek."

"Ah. Got it." Still smiling, he tiptoed out to the den and flopped onto the couch. They'd been up so late the night before that by the time he pulled up the blanket and closed his eyes; he'd fallen fast asleep

He awoke next to tapping on his shoulder. "Dad? What am I going to wear to school? I can't wear the same thing again."

He ran a hand down his face as he tried to shake the fog from his brain. "Ummm. We'll think of something." He sat up as his mind raced for an answer.

Lori appeared holding a Broncos sweatshirt, clearly having anticipated the clothes problem. When their eyes met, she blushed. It was adorable.

She said, "Asher, look what I have. Your favorite team. Why don't you wear this over your shirt? No one will know any better."

"Awesome!" Asher's eyes lit up, and he slipped the hoodie that was too big over his head. He loved the Broncos. "Thanks, Mrs. Went."

"Welcome. You look great." She ruffled his hair. "There's an extra toothbrush in Emily's bathroom. Bottom drawer. But for now, how about some scrambled eggs with cheese?"

"Yay. I'm starving!" Asher ran for the kitchen.

Deek took her hand and gave it a squeeze. "You saved the day. Again. Thank you, Lori."

"No problem." She looked around, and because the coast was clear, she leaned down and gave him a quick kiss. "You saved me from my sex-starved state, so now we're even. Feel free to use my shower. Breakfast will be waiting when you get out."

"Thanks."

Once the swinging door to the kitchen closed behind Lori, Deek flopped back onto the couch and smiled as he stared at the ceiling that needed a coat of paint.

Lori was one incredible woman.

At the Children's Museum, Lori helped the last kid in her group wash his hands free of clay, and then they joined the others as the instructor explained how the pottery oven worked. They'd all had a turn molding wet clay on the spinning wheel and were ready to bake their masterpieces. It looked like fun, and she was dying to try her hand at it. Now was her chance. She sat down and pressed the button with her foot to start the wheel spinning.

It'd been a great field trip so far, except that Mr. Raymond had asked her and Deek to team up. With a group of kids that didn't include Emily and Asher by their request. She couldn't blame them. Who'd want to go on a fun field trip with your parents watching your every move? And so far, the kids in their group had behaved themselves. And they'd made some pretty amazing things during their pot-throwing lessons.

She'd tried her best to avoid looking at Deek all day, but it was hard not to. He was so good with the kids, patiently showing them how to do all the projects they'd worked on so far. And they all adored him. He was such a great guy. Too bad she couldn't have him for herself. She needed to remember that.

Lori pressed her hands together as the slimy, wet hunk of clay slipped under her fingers. She was aiming for a vase, but things were quickly going crooked and awry. While she tried to make a correction, a big set of hands covered hers. Deek whispered in her ear, "It's all about pressure and angles."

"Very funny," she whispered under her breath. Memories of the last time he'd used those words made heat climb up her neck, and then swirl deep in her belly. His big, wet hands over hers weren't helping. Neither was the way he'd plastered his chest to her back. Or how his warm breath tickled her neck, sending shivers up her spine. Geez. She needed to get a grip. They were at a Children's Museum surrounded by kids. Besides, that had been a one-time thing, especially since Deek mentioned earlier that Annie was probably coming back soon for Asher's birthday.

"See? You're a natural, Lori." As Deek gently guided her hands with his, a beautiful pot appeared before her eyes.

"That's awesome. Now help me get it off in one piece, please."

Deek stood behind her with his big arms still wrapped around her and expertly removed the pot. When he backed up to take it to the oven, she missed his body heat. It made her shiver again.

Get a grip!

After she had washed her hands, she rejoined her group of kids. While the instructor explained the glazing process, she snuck another glance at Deek over their little heads. He was watching her too and smiled when their eyes met.

Ugh, she had it bad for him.

It made her a little sad. And more determined to get her head back in the chaperone game and ignore the sexy man across from her. She had a job to do, so she'd just do it. They were off to check out the climbing wall next. She needed to be on her toes to be sure no one got hurt.

After the field trip, on the way back to school, Lori stared out the window of the bus with her new pot in her lap. Thoughts of Deek's big wet hands on hers kept popping back into her mind all afternoon. She didn't dare look at him, or she'd blush for sure. Had they made a mistake by sleeping together? It didn't feel like a mistake. Her heart filled with joy every time she thought of Deek, but that was the problem. Sleeping with him had only made her want him even more.

The loud screech of the brakes announced they were finally back at the kids' school. Row by row, everyone slowly piled off the bus. There was still about an hour left of the school day, so the kids followed Mr. Raymond back to class, and all the parents were thanked and dismissed.

Lori silently walked alongside Deek to his big car, careful to leave plenty of distance so no one would get any ideas about the two of them. Once she was buckled in, and out of earshot of the other parents, she said, "It seems silly for both of us to go home and then come back in two hours after math club is over. Do you want me to pick up Asher and bring him to your house so at least one of us can get some work done today?"

Deek turned and stared into her eyes. "I think we should go to your house. I know of a fun way to fill those two hours."

He reached out and took her hand. "I've been thinking about it all day. What do you say?"

Her mind shouted, *Don't do it! You're only going to fall deeper for the man and get hurt.* Instead, she said, "My sister is there, so my place is out of the question." That wasn't a yes, and it wasn't a no. There was still time to come to her senses.

Frown lines creased his forehead. "I guess we could go to a hotel?"

"A hotel?" That seemed so...cheap. She pulled her hand from his. "No. You know what? We really shouldn't do this. Annie will be back in town soon. And last night was just you being nice, as usual, and taking pity on me." She'd give him an out. He had to choose Annie in the long run. Not her.

"Pity? Are you kidding me? It was the best night of my life." Deek quickly pulled a U-turn and headed the opposite way. "We'll go to my house. I should've thought of it first, but I don't..."

His hands fisted on the wheel as he seemed to wrangle with what to say next. As happy as she was to hear last night had been incredible for him too, something was wrong. She laid her hand over his. "What is it, Deek? We're still friends, aren't we? Despite last night?"

"Absolutely." He glanced her way and smiled again. Whatever demons had been bothering him before seemed to have been vanquished. "You're the only person I've ever met who I don't seem to annoy when I go into geek mode or don't catch on to obvious jokes."

She shook her head. "I think you're selling yourself short. You can be incredibly charming."

"And I think you're the *best* friend I've ever had, Lori. And I want it always to be that way. No matter what happens with Annie."

The warmth in his eyes was like a sweet caress to her heart. But then he'd mentioned Annie. "Me too, Deek." She leaned her head back against the seat and sighed. "Me too."

Was she about to make the biggest mistake in her life by falling completely in love with an irresistible man who just wanted to be her friend?

Or was it already too late?

11

SOMETIMES THINGS SEEM TOO GOOD TO BE TRUE. . . BUT MAYBE THEY AREN'T.

Deek wiped his sweaty palms on his jeans before he opened the door that led from his garage to the kitchen. Lori's jaw had dropped when she'd seen the front of the house, but she hadn't said anything except, "Wow." Why he cared so much if she liked his house, he wasn't sure, but he wanted her to.

He followed her as she entered his house. Lori looked hot dressed in jeans and tennis shoes. And she'd pulled her hair up in a ponytail. He liked the casual look.

"So this is the kitchen." He stood with his hands in his pockets and waited for her response.

"Wow." Lori smoothed her hand over the granite counter-tops as she looked around. "Just, wow, Deek."

Was that all the woman could say? He still couldn't tell if she liked his professional kitchen with miles of granite and top-notch appliances, or thought it was stupid and overly indulgent like Annie had. "I had them design it, so all the culinary toys I love to use in here have their place. To avoid clutter. They called them appliance garages, but that seems like a stupid name for a cabinet that holds a stand mixer or an espresso machine, right?"

"It makes sense to me." She turned her attention back to him and shrugged. "A garage is part of the house, but it's special use is to provide a place for a piece of equipment too."

She was right. He'd never thought of it that way. But he wished she'd tell him what she thought of his house, dammit. And what she was feeling for him. "Well, through here is the dining room." He started to cross the kitchen, and she caught up, still swiveling her head and taking it all in as they walked.

"I was just doing the math, Deek, and I think my entire house could fit in here. Seriously, you could bake for the whole town with all this counter space."

Was that a good thing or bad? "Yeah. I like to cook. And still have enough room to experiment."

She nodded as she took in the commercial freezer and refrigerator in the butler's pantry as they walked by. "You also have two of every appliance? Wait. Don't tell me. Let me guess. You're holding hostages in the basement? And you force them to make you a new funny T-shirt each day, right?"

They stopped walking, and he studied her face. "There's no basement."

She held up a finger. "But you don't deny the hostages?"

He gave her ponytail a light tug. "One of these days, I'm going to catch on to your sarcasm sooner, and then what will you do?"

"I'll have to up my game, I guess." She gave him a hug. "I love your house, Deek. I'm especially interested to see your bedroom. I'm half expecting framed superhero posters on the walls. Will I be disappointed?"

"Yes, because I have a whole room dedicated to my comic book memorabilia. And I might even let you see it. After." He took her hand and led her toward the stairs, pleased that Lori liked his house. He was going to show just how pleased he was with her as soon as he could get her naked again.

Lori flopped off of Deek and landed on her back beside him on the bed as she struggled for air. "You were right. Best way to kill a few hours, hands down." He'd topped his performance from the night before. She didn't think that'd even be possible.

He curled an arm around her waist and pulled her close. "You liked that last part, huh?"

Liked it? She'd loved it and wanted to do it again. "I really, really did. Thank you."

He tucked her head under his chin. "Welcome. But you nearly killed me. I'll be lucky if I can gather enough strength to show you the rest of my house before we have to go."

"Mmmmm." She closed her eyes and relished the feeling of being thoroughly sated. "As badly as I want to see your framed Wonder Woman poster, I'm not sure I have the strength for it either."

He tilted her chin up with a finger. "Of all the super-hero posters in the world, why would you guess that I have Wonder Woman?"

"My brother." She opened her eyes and smiled at the puzzled look on his face. "He once told me that since our mom wouldn't let him hang up pictures of naked girls in his room, Wonder Woman was the next best thing."

"True. She's really built. Like you." His hand slid gently all the way down the front of her body, paying extra attention to the good parts.

She could lie in bed with Deek all day. "I have to admit, that magic lasso of hers *is* pretty amazing. Oh, and that invisible plane? I think I need one of those."

Deek nodded as he continued to caress her skin. "But what good did having an invisible plane do when you could see her sitting inside flying it?"

"You're being too literal. The guy who thought her up, and you *know* it was a man, wouldn't dream of hiding her curves when she was doing something as sexy as flying a jet. He'd want everyone to share in his fantasy woman…whatever she does, right?"

"Ah. I see your point." He leaned down and kissed her. "And for the record, I think you are ten times sexier than she is. But I wouldn't mind seeing what we could do with that magic lasso."

"Maybe you should do some research and then get back to me."

"Deal." Deek swiped a piece of fallen hair behind her ear. "Honestly, I would've never guessed you'd be this fun in bed."

Never guessed? Why wouldn't she be fun in bed?

He'd picked at an open sore. Her husband sometimes wanted her to be more adventurous, but certain things were just off-limits. It'd always made her wonder if that was why he cheated with Mel.

"Maybe we better go get the kids." She tried to roll away, but Deek held her tight.

"Wait. What did I say?"

She huffed out a breath. He couldn't have known. Taking it out on him wasn't fair. "I'm sorry. It's just that Joe used to accuse me of being a prude sometimes, especially after Emily was born."

"Seriously?" Deek's forehead rumpled. "I haven't been with anyone who seems to enjoy sex as much as you do. And I love how vocal you are about it."

Leave it to Deek to make her feel better. "That's new for me. And totally your fault."

"It makes me happy to make you happy, Lori. But have I asked you to do anything you're uncomfortable with?"

"No." God, he was so cute. "Joe was an adrenaline junkie. He liked the thrill of having sex in places that weren't always the most comfortable, or that would be mortifying to me if we got caught. I think he actually hoped we would get caught sometimes."

"That was part of the thrill? To embarrass you?"

"I can't say I totally ever knew for sure. But give me a bed over a tree trunk at my back any day. I was usually the one who ended up with the scrapes and bruises."

"Ouch." Deek leaned over and kissed her again. Slowly, deeply, and with so much tenderness, it felt like her heart might explode.

After he had ended the kiss, he whispered, "Joe didn't appreciate what he had. You make me want to spend every waking moment with you. You're incredibly beautiful, sexy, sweet, funny, and the kindest woman I've ever met. Not to mention you're the loudest woman I've ever known in bed."

Her heart hurt with all her pent-up feelings for him. But she'd sworn she wouldn't tell him how she really felt about him. He had a deep moral need to get Annie back for Asher that she'd never want him to betray in himself. And she couldn't be the one standing in Asher's way of having that. "I think you're one of the nicest guys I've ever met. It's just a bonus you're so damn good in bed. How long before Annie returns and I get the boot?"

She would not cry. No matter what he said, she'd plaster on a smile.

"The boot? That sounds so...cold." Deek rolled onto his back and threw his arm over his face. "You make it ten times harder for me to do the right thing for Asher."

That was exactly what she didn't want. He needed to be sure what and who he wanted to choose. He might blame her later for not staying true to his gut. "You probably don't want me, Deek. I mean in bed, sure, we get along fantastic there, but I'm a person who has a very hard time trusting."

"Yet all I can think about is how much I do want you. And I think you want me too. I can't figure out why you won't tell me how you feel about me and put me out of my misery."

Dammit. Should she tell him how she felt? He was already doubting without her help. "Of course, if you were free, I'd want to be with you, Deek. But you're not. You love Annie."

"I didn't think I was free a couple of weeks ago. But now?" He groaned. "Make my decision easier. Tell me why you have trust issues and how much I don't want to be with you."

She drew a deep breath. She hated the painful memories that talking about it brought. "My father cheated on my mom, and while they're back together now, that's only happened recently. I have deep scars from watching my mom deal with that. They were apart for over twenty years, and he wasn't a hands-on father. My mom raised us. When Joe cheated on me, I think it did some damage I'm not sure I can ever repair. It was like my father leaving us all over again, but worse." All that was true, but she'd make an exception and take a chance with Deek in a heartbeat. But only if he figured out on his own that he wanted her and Emily more than Annie—and could live with that choice.

She didn't want him to make an impulsive decision and always wonder if he still loved Annie. Sharing her man with another woman would never happen again if she could help it.

Deek rolled over and faced her. "I have to do anything I can to make Asher's home complete, right? And that means living with both of his parents. It's the right thing to do. Isn't it?"

She got out of bed and started searching for her clothes. They needed to pick up the kids soon. "You have to do what your heart thinks is right, Deek. Not out of obligation, but for love. If you're happy, then Asher will be happy, no matter what you choose to do. Because *you* love him and that's all he really needs. To be loved by someone."

Deek propped his head up on his hand. "Do you believe that? Just because you love Emily, she'll be fine?"

"I have to." She pulled her sweater over her head, then tugged up her jeans. "Joe's never coming back."

"Would you have taken him back if he hadn't died?"

"I've asked myself that question a hundred times." She sat on the edge of the bed and tied her shoes. When she was done, she turned to Deek. "And every time, the answer is no. Even though I loved him with all my heart, I wouldn't have taken him back. I need a man who respects me enough to be faithful to me. Not only physically," she leaned over and patted his heart, "but here too. All this real estate has to belong to only me. Listen to your heart, Deek."

There. She'd said as much as she was going to say. He'd had such a crappy childhood with a parent who'd ignored him so Deek might pick Annie out of sheer obligation. Or maybe he'd catch a clue and realize that together, she and Deek could give Emily and Asher a great family.

She got up to head for the bathroom, but Deek caught her hand to stop her. "I never answered your question. We only have a week before Asher's birthday. So I'd understand if you'd rather not sleep together anymore. We could go back to just being friends. I plan to marry Annie as soon as she says yes, and I don't want to hurt you, Lori."

Or one could look at it as a one-week opportunity to show him that she was the better choice for him. "I'd rather try to make it the best week of our lives if it's all the same to you. You could look into that magic lasso thing."

A slow-growing smile lit his face. "I could *absolutely* do that."

"Okay. Then it's settled." One week wasn't much time. But it was all she had. She'd make the best of it. And in the end, she'd either get the opportunity to get to know the man of her dreams better or get handed another broken heart.

12

LET THE GAMES BEGIN.

Lori yawned into her coffee cup as she tapped away on her keyboard with her free hand. She'd been at Shelby and Jo's restaurant for hours and still wasn't close to where she needed to be work- and school-wise. She needed to catch up on her matchmaking business responsibilities, take a quiz in her economics class, and then she needed to figure out how she and Deek could grab some alone time. The clock was ticking. Annie was due back in six days.

After she'd slept on her deal with Deek, she'd awoken with trepidation in her heart. Was she trying to steal another woman's man? She'd never do that on purpose. Never do what her former best friend had done by sleeping with Joe.

Annie had told Deek to sleep with other women, so they'd know for sure it was right for them to settle down. So, it was all honest and fair. She hoped.

The door opened, and a cool breeze accompanied Shelby inside. She lifted a hand in greeting and then made a beeline for the brownies Jo had made for them. After stuffing one into her mouth, she made her way to Lori's table.

"Hey there, stranger." Shelby shrugged out of her coat. "I guess you've recovered from Monday night's fiasco? I refunded Jason's money and purged him from the files, by the way."

"Thanks." Lori had almost forgotten about Jason. And it was only Wednesday. "Deek and I are working on a way to dig a little deeper into our clients' backgrounds. I'll let you know what we come up with."

Shelby lifted a brow. "Ms. I-do-everything-on-paper when I met you is going to help solve a cyber problem?"

"Deek's a genius with computers." And in bed, but she wasn't going to share that part with Shelby just yet.

"Why are you blushing?" Her sister-in-law leaned closer and whispered, "You slept with him. Didn't you?"

Of all the attributes to have, why blushing? Rachel didn't have it. "Maybe."

Shelby waited for the details like a puppy waiting for a treat. All smiles and wiggles of excitement. "Come on, Lori. Spill. I'm a boring, pregnant, married woman. I need to live vicariously through you."

"You haven't even been married for a year yet. I'm sure you have plenty of sex with my brother that I don't want to hear about."

"True." She smiled like a cat who just scored a bowl of cream. "I'm glad Deek stumbled into Rachel's party last weekend. I like him. A lot. And if Nick knew I told you this, he'd kill me, but he really liked him too. He said it was too soon to be sure Deek wouldn't break your heart. But if he did, Nick thought he could still take the guy, even though Deek's built. Nick is so protective of you; it's cute. I love that about him."

She loved her brother too, but sometimes his protectiveness could be cloying. "Nick isn't going to have to beat anyone up. I might be doing that to myself all on my own."

"What do you mean?" Shelby's smile instantly disappeared.

After Lori had explained the situation with Deek and Annie, she sat back and waited for Shelby's take on the matter. It was important what her sister-in-law thought. Rachel's reaction to the whole situation had been to go for it, and then she went online and bought Lori better lingerie. It was due in by Friday. She'd always been Rachel's conscience, not the other way around.

Shelby leaned back and blew out a long breath. "First, there's a kid involved here, so could you see yourself marrying Deek and therefore becoming Asher's stepmother one day?"

"Yes. I realize Deek and I haven't known each other well for very long, but it was like this with Joe too. My heart knew right away. Deek and Joe are the only two people that's ever happened with. And Asher's a great kid. I'm already fond of him."

"Yeah. I remember you saying that about Joe." Shelby's expression grew pensive. "So Deek told you how he felt about you first, but what did he say when you said he wasn't free to be with you because he loved Annie?"

What had he said about that? "Something like he thought he was taken, but then he met me."

"Hmmmm. So it's possible he doesn't even love Annie romantically, and he's just doing his duty?"

Lori finished off her coffee as she considered that thought. She'd never heard him actually say he loved her. Just that he was sure Annie loved them, in her own way. "I don't know, but he said I was making it ten times harder to do the right thing for Asher. That's the crux of all of this. Deek feels duty bound to provide Asher a home, complete with both of his parents. I'm not sure I should get in the middle of something he believes so strongly about."

Shelby shrugged. "Yeah. Because the alternative is that you're miserable without him, Deek's miserable because he'd rather be with you, and Asher could end up living in a home with a father who'd settled, and a mother who'd rather be out digging in the dirt than be with her son and husband. So it's better you step away, then everyone can be miserable all around."

Shelby was just the person she needed to hear say that. "So you don't think I'm a home-wrecker?"

"No. I think you're a woman with a huge heart who's falling in love. And any man who says he wants to spend every waking moment with you is a man who sounds happy. Because of you. And I know you'd be the best stepmother any kid could ask for. So I'll wish you luck."

Lori's heart felt light as a feather again. "Thank you—"

"Wait." Shelby cut her off. "But if you move forward with this plan, you'll also need to be prepared for if it doesn't work out all happy rainbows and unicorns. Deek might have to put Asher first and do what he thinks is best for his son. And if that's what he chooses, you have to be prepared to walk away and let him live with his choice."

That was a sobering scenario. But Shelby was right. "I'm fully prepared to have my heart bludgeoned."

"Bludgeoned?" Shelby winced. "That's a harsh word, but probably just how it'd feel. If that happens, I'll bring the chocolate and wine. Then we'll hate on men while you get drunk and I get even fatter."

"That's assuming I'd share the chocolate. And that's not a given."

"You underestimate me." She reached into her purse and pulled out a chocolate bar. "I never leave home without one. And a barf bag."

Lori smiled, grateful she had such a wonderful support system. Life was too short to be afraid of another heartbreak. And commitment again. She'd have to work on that one as she went along.

So, she'd finish up her work and then find an excuse to see Deek later. Maybe she'd invite him over for dinner. Or better yet, talk him into cooking for them in that beautiful kitchen he claimed to love to use.

She hadn't thought of that before. That if she and Deek ended up together, she might never have to cook on a daily basis again. Talk about icing on the cake.

Deek glanced at the time on his computer screen. Annie was supposed to call, but he'd taken Lori's advice and decided to quit reminding Annie to talk to her son. Since they'd just talked on Monday, maybe Asher wouldn't be too disappointed if she forgot.

He leaned back in his chair and ran the terms of the deal he'd make with Annie in order to give her the money for the dig. He'd reiterated the option of marriage again, but hadn't made it a requirement for the money. Her visits home were nonnegotiable, but if Annie didn't want to marry him, he could live with that now.

He'd ask one more time when she got home and tell her it'd be the last. He didn't want to be left hanging anymore. He and Asher didn't deserve to be treated like that.

Annie's main passion in life was archeology. She'd agreed that this would be her only dig, and then she'd take a museum job after she returned. Which might mean they'd have to move, but he could work from anywhere. However, anywhere but Denver meant he'd never see Lori again. But if they stayed, could he see her every day as just friends and not want her as badly as he wanted her now? He'd thought about her twenty-five times since he'd woken up.

He'd never done that with Annie.

Or maybe he had when he and Annie had first started dating in college. Maybe Lori was just something shiny and new, and he was making a mistake leading her on. But it didn't feel like a mistake. It felt…right.

His phone dinged with a text that brought him out of his uncertain haze. He picked it up, hoping it was Annie.

Even better, it was Lori.

Hey, Chef Deek. What's cooking for dinner at your house tonight?

He smiled. *Hi, princess. Nothing fit for royalty. I'm serving slop.*

Slop???? Served in wooden troughs? And eaten with your hands? Like Henry the VIII style? I guess if it was good enough for a king, I could hang with that.

No. As in sloppy Joes for ten rowdy Cub Scouts. It'll look like a pigsty around here after they go home. Do princesses ever get on their knees and scrub floors?

You've seen what I do best on my knees. And it isn't cleaning.

Yes. Quite memorable. How about tomorrow night? I'll cook whatever you guys want.

Can't. Emily has her soccer team coming over for dinner. We have to come up with a fundraiser before the season starts. Those out-of-town trips aren't in our budget.

He hated how Lori had to struggle with money, school, and work. She deserved a break, not one more task to add to her life. *I'd be happy to fund Emily's soccer trips.*

Nope. That's nice of you, but we'll work it out. The only thing I'll let you buy me is dinner. How about Friday?

Annie wanted a million bucks for a dig, and all Lori asked of him was dinner. *Absolutely. Asher just asked if he could spend the night at his friend John's house, so you and I could have a spend-the-night too.*

Perfect. It's supposed to snow again on Friday, so we might have to work around the weather.

I've been dying to try out my new sous vide machine. Want me to make you the best steak you've ever had right here? Then after, we can watch a movie in my home theater. Six thirty work?

Yes. I'll pack my new sexy lingerie. And my kneepads. :0)

He smiled as visions of Lori in sexy lingerie filled his mind. Friday couldn't come fast enough for him.

Lori was still trying to decide which of her new lingerie to pack on Friday afternoon when Rachel flopped onto Lori's bed. "What are we telling Emily about why you're not coming home tonight?"

"I couldn't bear to lie to her, so Mom is going to call and invite her for a sleepover in a bit."

Rachel's eyebrow arched. "You told Mom you're having a sex date and won't be home until tomorrow?"

"No!" Lori threw a pillow at Rachel. "And it's not a sex date. I mean, there will be lots of that, but we're having dinner and watching a movie too."

"What *are* we telling Mom?" Rachel threw the pillow back, even harder.

"Nothing. If all goes well. I mentioned Emily would love an invite, and Mom was super excited to have her. I told her I had a date, so you'd be here when she picks Em up at seven. Emily is never ready to end the fun before eleven the next morning, so I'll pick her up on my way home, and Mom will never be the wiser."

Rachel laughed. "You're a grown-up now, and could tell Mom the truth. She knows we have sex sometimes. You're just a whole lot louder about it than me."

"You heard that the other night?" Heat rose up Lori's neck. She had to look away before her sister saw the full-out blush.

"The neighbors must've heard it. I'm sure they said, 'Hallelujah! Lori is finally getting some!' Then they probably put their earbuds in and cranked the music like I did. You're lucky Emily and Asher sleep like the dead."

Mortified, she slumped down on the edge of the bed. "It's just that Deek is a fantastic lover. It's like you feel safe to just…let go."

"Obviously." Rachel rolled onto her back and stared at the ceiling. "It's the same with Marcello and me. You made me miss him. And that. I finally answered when he called this afternoon."

"And?" Lori stood to finish packing. "Did you tell him about the babies?"

"No. Not yet. I just missed him and wanted to talk. He said he loved me, and as soon as his movie wraps, he wants to spend a whole month with me. He said he's already cleared his calendar. No easy feat for him."

"Did you tell him you loved him too?"

"I tried. But I couldn't. I've never told any man I love him." Rachel closed her eyes, but her tears leaked out anyway. "Damn these pregnancy hormones. They've turned me into a blubbering weakling."

"Crying doesn't make you weak." Lori sat down beside her sister again. "And neither does confessing your love for someone. It can actually be freeing."

"Maybe. But what if he's just saying that? What if he's just upset because I left him? He said once that no one has ever broken up with him. He's always the one who does it first."

"I don't think he would have made all the effort to spend a month with you just because he has a bruised ego."

"I guess." Rachel shrugged. "Have you told Deek you're falling in love with him yet?"

"No. I don't want to put any more pressure on him. He needs to decide who he wants. Me or Annie." And she needed to decide on the sexy blue undies or the black really sexy ones Rachel picked out as a challenge. Black it was.

"Or, you're just as afraid to do it as I am." Rachel wiped away her tears and rolled off the bed. "You only have a few more days to state your case. Telling him you love him might help him decide what to do. And you never know. It might be FREEING."

"Very funny," Lori called out to her sister's retreating back. "Call Marcello tonight and tell him, Rachel. I promise you won't be any less of a bad-ass woman in the morning."

Her sister stopped in the doorway and glanced over her shoulder. "But I will always be a bigger bad-ass than you."

"That's debatable." Lori held a hand out toward her bag. "I just packed the black undies. And I'm the one having a sex date tonight. Not you."

"Seems I've been knocked off my throne. By a Goody Two-shoes, no less." Rachel chuckled all the way to the den.

Lori shook her head as she zipped up her bag. She wasn't a Goody Two-shoes. Well, sometimes, but not tonight. She was going to spend the night with a sexy man and do all kinds of naughty and fun things. But something Rachel said still bugged her. She was right—with limited time to fight for Deek, she needed to tell him how she felt about him. So she would. Maybe while wearing the sexy black undies for extra courage.

13

WHEN THE AX FALLS, THE TRUTH COMES OUT.

"This looks wonderful, Deek." Lori smiled at the plate Deek had just placed before her.

He hoped she'd like it. They'd had stuffed mushroom appetizers and were on their second glass of wine, and he couldn't remember a more enjoyable dinner date. He'd thought they'd use the fancy dining room that he never used, but when he started to set the table, she said she'd be just as comfortable at the bar in the kitchen where she'd watched him cook for the last hour. It was nice to have the company and conversation as he chopped and sautéed.

He took a seat next to Lori and glanced at her just as she took her first bite of the steak. It was ridiculous how much he hoped she'd like it.

She closed her eyes and moaned. "Mmmmmmm, Deek. This is incredible."

Relieved the steak had passed the test, he took his first bite and made an involuntary noise that sounded just like hers. He'd impressed himself. "I'm glad these turned out, being the first time I've used that machine. And especially since the snow decided to hold off until later and we could have gone to a restaurant. I'll make it up to you. Maybe tomorrow?"

Lori shook her head as she chewed. "This is better than any restaurant steak I've ever had. But dinner tomorrow sounds great. No matter where we end up having it."

He smiled as he sipped his wine. Lori was such an easy person to be with. "How did the soccer fundraising summit go last night? Did the girls come up with a plan?"

"Yes. Be prepared for Emily to hit you up to buy candy bars very soon. And don't you dare buy a whole case or anything. She needs to understand it takes work to pay for what she wants in life."

"How many come in a case?" He speared an asparagus and popped it into his mouth. He hated vegetables but made himself eat them.

"Like twenty-four or something." Lori slathered more butter and sour cream onto her baked potato, then passed the condiments to him. "She's going to have to sell quite a few cases, but it's doable."

Then he'd buy twenty candy bars, but he wouldn't mention it now. "Maybe Asher can help her. I just realized I've never made him work for anything. That's probably not good."

"There's not only one way to raise kids. And every kid is different, so I suppose you have to adjust the plan as you go."

Adjust the plan as you go? Could he adjust his plans for Asher when it came to Annie? Maybe he was planning and hoping too much for something that just wasn't going to work out. She hadn't called since last Monday. "Speaking of plans and kids, I booked that new laser tag place for Asher's party next Saturday. I figured we'd just have something small on Tuesday here, for his actual birthday. Maybe you guys could come for cake?"

Lori blinked at him for a moment before she laid her fork down. "I'm not sure Annie would appreciate us, more specifically me, being here. We're sleeping together, and women can sense those things."

"Oh. Right." He stabbed three more asparagus spears to finish them off so he wouldn't have to look at them anymore. "That is if Annie even shows up. I haven't heard one way or the other."

"We'll play Tuesday by ear. So after we watch a movie, can I see your comic memorabilia room?"

She was changing the subject. Why was he talking about Annie with Lori anyway? It was just that he felt like he could talk to her about anything. "Yes. And I have a piece that I think you'll especially enjoy."

"Can't wait. What movie did you have in mind for us?" Lori smiled, and the tension he'd just caused seemed to evaporate.

"I doubt you're an X-Men fan, so it'll be ladies' choice."

"I think Wolverine is pretty damn hot." Lori shrugged. "I could watch him without his shirt on all night long."

"Then forget it. We'll watch a romantic comedy." He didn't want her ogling anyone but him. Was that jealousy? He'd never been jealous before.

"That'd be great too." Lori smiled as she finished off her steak.

After a few more minutes of enjoying their food in comfortable silence, a thought occurred to him. "Did you just trick me into watching a romantic comedy?"

"Yes." Lori stood and took her empty plate to the sink. "That you figured it out is progress. But I actually do like a good X-Men movie from time to time, so I'll be happy with whatever we watch."

Man, she really was the perfect woman.

"Leave the dishes. I haven't told you this, but I have a housekeeper during the week. She'll get them in the morning."

"Seriously?" Lori spun around. "That would be my dream. To never scrub a dish or a toilet again as long as I live. What other great surprises does this place come with?"

He stood and slid his arms around her waist. "There are indoor and outdoor pools and hot tubs that I'd hoped to show you a bit later, a ten-seat movie theater, a bar complete with a dance floor, not that I dance, a sauna off the gym, and my favorite place in the house, the video game room. I have an original Pac-Man machine."

"Pac-Man?" She laid a quick kiss on his lips. "I used to love that game. I bet living here is like living in Disneyland."

"That was the idea." It wasn't nearly as fun to have all those great things without someone who appreciated them, though. "Let's go pick something out to watch."

He took her hand and led her to the theater. When they passed by his comic book room, he punched in the code to unlock the door. "Since we're here. Have a quick look."

"You keep whatever's in there locked up?" she asked.

"Yeah. Mostly because Asher loves this room but rarely has clean hands. Some of this is pretty valuable." He hit the main switch, and the whole room lit up. Everything had lighting to show it off at its best. Even the glass cases were esthetically lit where the most prized of his comic books lived.

Lori's eyes went wide. "I've never seen anything like this." She slowly walked around the room, studying all the pieces. When she got to the Wonder Woman section that took up a larger amount of space because he'd always thought she was the sexiest superhero there was, Lori stopped and crossed her arms. "Uh-huh. Just as I suspected." Then she spotted the replica of the Wonder Woman plane, and her hands shot out to pick it up.

But then Lori stopped herself and asked, "May I touch this? My hands are clean. I swear."

"Of course you can." He moved behind her and lifted the glass plane, complete with a Wonder Woman action figure inside, and handed it to her. "You remind me of her. Sexy, strong, and good to the core."

After she studied the plane for a moment, she gently put it back. Then she snuggled her curvy body against his as she wrapped her arms around his neck. "And I think you're even better to look at than Wolverine without his shirt. Sexier, smarter, and lots nicer than any of the X-Men."

He'd wanted to tell her he was falling in love with her, but he'd just sent an e-mail to Annie last Sunday night asking if she'd reconsider marrying him along with all the other absolute requirements for him to fund her dig. That was before he'd slept with Lori and realized how much more he wanted from her than just her friendship. If only he knew for sure that Lori felt as strongly for him as he did for her…

But then what?

He had no idea what the hell he was going to do when Annie got back. That is if she ever came back.

Lori laughed at the romantic comedy playing on the twelve-foot-tall screen. She was snuggled up against Deek's side on the leather reclining seats and enjoying the movie immensely. His theater was awesome, with a top-notch sound system, a tiered floor, so every seat in the place was a good one, and he even had a stocked bar so they could drink wine while they watched. She'd sort of lost count of how many glasses she'd had, but the warm and fuzzy buzz she had was a pleasant one.

When she glanced up at him, still impressed he'd worn a button-down shirt for their date, that same little crease was still on his forehead. Right between his eyes. It had formed in the Wonder Woman room. That was what she'd always think of that room as, now that he'd compared her to a superhero. She whispered, "Everything okay?"

"Yeah. Fine." He smiled, but it was forced.

Something was bothering him, so she leaned across his chest and found the remote to pause the movie. Then she crawled onto his lap and cupped his face in her hands. "Then why is this worry line still here?" She traced it with a finger.

"I've just got a lot on my mind. That's all." He kissed her so sweetly it made her sigh.

When he was done and had left her lips tingling for more, he said, "Can I interest you in skinny-dipping in the pool when this is over? I've never done that with anyone, and I'd really like you to be the first."

"I'd be honored to christen your pool with our nakedness." The frown line had disappeared on his forehead. Had he been worried about asking to skinny-dip? "But how about I challenge you to a Pac-Man tournament first? Loser has to make breakfast in the morning."

He shook his head. "You don't want to do that, Lori. I'm damn good at that game."

"So am I." She took his hand and pulled him out of the seat. "We were stationed at this base when I was first married to Joe. We were pretty poor, and Joe was overseas, so the only thing the wives could afford to do on a Friday night was go to the rec center. They had free movies, one-dollar beers, and cheap hot dogs."

When they got to the hallway, she asked, "Which way?"

"This way." He pointed down a long hall.

It was hard to keep her bearings straight.

He turned her shoulders in the right direction, and when they set out across the travertine-tiled floor, he said, "So back to dollar beers and hot dogs…"

"Oh yeah, well they rigged up the video games to play for free too, but they were all the really old ones. Nothing like they have now, and Pac-Man was one of them. I was the reigning champ for a solid year. And then we moved."

He swung his arm over her shoulder. "Were you always this agreeable? Happy with so little? I was broke growing up and swore I'd never be poor again. I hated it."

"That explains this house. But it was what it was. I could mope about it like some of the other wives did, or I could embrace it and become a champion at something."

He shook his head. "Joe was a lucky guy."

She sighed. Joe must've not felt the same, or why would he have ever cheated on her? She needed to quit having thoughts like that if she was ever going to be able to move on and trust again.

Luckily, they'd arrived at the game room, and Deek was busy turning on lights so she wouldn't have to comment.

She took in all the different machines as he crossed to the rear. He had Skee Ball, high-tech team driving games, a motorcycle game a person could ride, classic pinball machines, and the dancing one Emily loved to try to keep up with. If it weren't for the promise of skinny-dipping later, she'd happily spend the rest of the evening in the arcade.

Deek leaned down to turn on the Pac-Man machine. "Be prepared to give up your title, princess. I see bacon grease and egg shells in your near future."

"You're dreaming, pal." She gave him a shoulder bump. "Best two out of three?"

"You got it." He held his hand out. "Ladies first."

She pushed the button, and the game began. She was a little rusty at first, but it came right back. Like riding a bike. "I think I'd like my breakfast served to me in bed in the morning."

"Don't get too cocky." Deek snuggled up against her back and watched over her shoulder as she racked up points. When she reached the first bonus round, he leaned down and nibbled on her neck. "Nice. But still amateur level."

"Yeah. Then why are you trying so hard to distract me?"

He moved his hands to her breasts and squeezed. "You're the distracting one here. Don't mind me."

She smiled while doing her best to ignore his large hands caressing and teasing her body. She was hanging in, until he snuggled his hard crotch against her rear end, reminding her how much she wanted him too.

He whispered, "Watching how intense you are while playing my favorite game is seriously sexy. How about I concede right now so I can have you on top of this machine?"

She was just about to throw in the towel when a feminine voice called out, "Deek?"

"Annie?" His hands quickly snapped to his sides before he turned around. "What are you doing here?"

Annie was back? Crap!

Her time to win Deek back had just run out.

14

LEARNING TO TRUST AGAIN IS HARD TO DO WHEN THE WORLD KEEPS PITCHING YOU CURVE BALLS.

Lori's heart nearly beat out of her chest with nerves. Deek asked Annie what she was doing here, and Lori was dying to know the answer too. He hadn't been expecting her until Asher's birthday, and not even then for sure.

"Apparently interrupting something fun," Annie's monotone voice answered.

Deek still stood in front of Lori, as if he was hiding her. She didn't know what his plan was, but she poked him in the back to spur him on.

"Oh." He stepped aside and held his hand out toward her. "This is my friend Lori. We were just playing some video games. How did you get in?"

Annie held up a key. "You gave me this, remember? And the gate code." Her eyes shifted to Lori. "He said he built this house for *me*."

Annie was clearly marking her territory. One she'd had little or no desire to claim until that moment.

Lori glanced at Deek. The look of sheer terror on his face reminded her of Emily whenever she got caught with her hand in the cookie jar right before dinner. But surely he'd say something. Explain to Annie that things have changed. And that he was taking her advice and dating other women.

Deek just stood there with his hands shoved into his pockets. Totally flummoxed. Wasn't he going to remind Annie about how they could see other people?

Well, she wasn't going to pretend this wasn't a date. They were adults and could all be civil about the awkward situation.

Lori stepped forward and held out her hand. "I'm Emily's mom. She and Asher are in the same class at school."

Annie stared at Lori's hand for a moment before she finally reached out and shook it. "Annie." She turned to Deek. "If I'm still welcome here, then I think I'll go on up to *our* room and go to bed. I've been traveling all day, and I'm beat."

Deek's jaw flopped opened and closed like a fish out of water as he looked back and forth between her and Annie. "Of course you're welcome. Asher will be thrilled to see you. He's at a sleepover but will be home in the morning. And Lori was just leaving anyway."

Just leaving?

Before she could say anything, Annie's eyes locked with hers again and she said, "Good. Then Deek and I can have some privacy to celebrate. I came home to accept his proposal. He asked me to *marry* him last Monday." Annie's gaze shifted back to his. "We'll do it next week. At the courthouse, if that works. Goodbye, Lori." Then she turned and walked out of the arcade.

All the air whooshed from Lori's lungs. Annie was accepting his marriage proposal?

She looked up at Deek as she tried to draw enough air to speak. "You asked her to marry you on Monday?" That was the day they'd first slept together. How could he do that to her?

How could she have been so wrong about him? She thought he was different. Not the type to play two women at once so he could get laid.

Like Joe had done to her.

"No. Yes, maybe. I mean she opened the e-mail on Monday, I suppose. This is all happening too fast." Deek shook his head. "I can explain, Lori. I'm just not sure what to do here."

Not sure what to do? Yeah, she'd been an idiot to open up her heart again. "Never mind, Deek. I was *just leaving*, right?"

He ran a hand down his face. "I'm not good at confrontation. I can't find the right words as fast as she can."

"What if she'd come in five minutes later? When you were showing me how much you wanted me? Would you have still told her I was just your *friend*?"

He lifted his hand's palms up and then let them fall helplessly by his sides. "I honestly don't know what I would've said. But I didn't mean to hurt—"

She held up her hand to stop him. "Never mind, Deek. You made your choice. Have a nice life."

She headed for the front door, blinking back her tears.

"Wait." Deek caught up with her and slipped his hand around her arm to stop her. "Can you just give me a minute to think? I don't know what the hell I'm supposed to do. This wasn't supposed to happen like this."

Lori stared into his eyes. Her heart, still carrying the scars Joe had left on it, shattered into a million pieces. "That you don't know what to do means you should probably go upstairs. Annie's waiting for you." She yanked her arm out of his grasp. Her only goal was to get to her car before she fell completely apart.

When she got to the foyer to grab her coat and bag, Annie stood at the bottom of the steps with a triumphant grin on her face. "Buh-bye, now."

Annie had to have heard their whole conversation. And who knew how long Annie had been standing behind them in the arcade before she'd said something?

Asher's mother wasn't as nerdy and innocent as Deek made her out to be. She'd known exactly what she'd been doing.

And she'd won Deek's love, even though she didn't deserve it.

Lori was almost all the way to the door before she stopped and turned around. She marched back toward Annie and got in her face, "If you're just using him for his money so you can go play in the dirt rather than grow up and be Asher's mother, then at least have the decency not to marry him. Take the money, but let him move on."

Annie raised a brow. "And let you win? Not happening, loser. And Asher won't be playing with Emily anymore either. Now get out of my house."

Rage fisted her hands. It took all her self-control to keep them at her sides. "Don't even think about dragging the kids into this, or I'll be sure to tell Deek what you really are, Annie."

She laughed. "Thanks for letting me in on your plan. All I'll have to do now is run some interference. He won't believe a word you say because Deek *loves* me. Not you. Get over it." Annie turned and walked up the steps. "There's nothing uglier than a bitter woman, Lori."

A bitter woman? She refused to be one. She'd known going in this could happen. But it didn't mean her heart hadn't just been destroyed because it had. She was pretty sure it'd never be the same again.

She left, slamming the big wooden door behind her as she made her way to her car in the driveway. She turned around and took one last look at the majestic Tuscan-style home. Deek stood in his study window. He slowly lifted a hand.

Screw holding back her tears until she got to the car. She let them fall as freely as the snowflakes that were coming down on her head. Let him see how much he'd hurt her.

And as she'd promised Shelby, Lori would walk away and let Deek live with the decision he'd just made.

While she lost all faith in men.

After Lori's car had disappeared down the drive, Deek flopped into his desk chair. He'd seen that look in Annie's eyes. The one she got when she was angry enough to start breaking things. She didn't lose control often, but when she did, it wasn't pretty. He hadn't wanted Lori to be Annie's target.

He held his head in his hands as he counted all the ways he'd screwed that up. He'd asked Annie to marry him fifteen times, and she'd never accepted. Until now. It had thrown him off and confused him. And how could he have told her she wasn't welcome in her own home? As far as he was concerned, it was her home too, just not on paper. He didn't want to make her so mad that she left before Asher could see her.

"Deek? Are you coming to bed?" Annie stood in the doorway.

He lifted his head. "No. Not yet. I have some work to catch up on." The last thing he wanted to do was sleep with Annie when twenty minutes ago he was about to sleep with Lori. He needed to sort things out first.

Annie crossed her arms. "It didn't look like you were too worried about work while you and Lori were in the arcade."

Crap. He wished everyone would leave him alone so he could think.

He hated to lie, but he didn't know what else to do. "I just checked my e-mail. I need to make a critical fix." Next week. Not that she needed to know that.

"Okay. But I've been asking around about Lori this past week. I think she's just using you for your money."

What? That wasn't true. "Lori would never do that, Annie."

She let out a long sigh. "You know it's happened before. It's because you trust people too easily. And you don't pick up on subtle behaviors. You've fallen prey *again*, Deek. But we won't have to worry about that anymore, once we're married." She stepped farther inside and stopped in front of his desk. "And Asher will finally have the family he deserves, right?"

That was the argument he'd given her for years about Asher. And why they should be married. Asher deserved to have both of his parents. It was their duty to their son. "But why now, Annie?"

She blinked at him. "Because it's clear you and Asher need me. Look at the mistake you were just about to make with that woman. You always said I was strong where you were weak and vice versa."

He used to think that. And it was true on paper. But it didn't feel as true anymore. "Okay. I have to get this done." And he hated that she didn't say it was because she finally realized that she loved him.

"Good night, Deek. Don't stay up too late."

"Okay. Night."

He waited until she was out the door before he picked up his phone. Lori should be home by now. But what was he going to say? He started to tap out a text telling her they'd work everything out but stopped. What was he doing? Annie was back, and she was finally going to marry him. It was what he'd wanted for the last seven years.

He erased his text and tossed his phone aside.

Did he still love Annie? He'd always love her because she was Asher's mother, but did he love her as much as he'd envisioned he could love Lori? What if he was making the biggest mistake of his life?

He picked up the phone again.

Just wanted to be sure you made it home okay.

He crossed his arms and laid his head down as he waited for her reply. When one didn't come after a half hour, he began to worry. She'd been crying and upset. And the roads were slick. What if something had happened to her? He'd have to go over there to be sure she was okay.

Finally, his phone chimed.

I'm home.

I'm sorry, Lori. And I'm sleeping on the couch tonight. Just wanted you to know.

Twenty more minutes had passed before she wrote back. *Thank you. I hope Asher and Emily can remain friends even if we can't*

Of course they can. And I hope we can too

Nope. Can't have it both ways. Goodbye.

Dammit! He'd lost her friendship too? She'd filled a void in his life he hadn't even known was there until he'd met her.

He threw his phone on his desktop and rubbed his eyes. He had a raging headache. And in the morning, he was going to have to talk to Annie again.

And tell her what?

Lori had been crying so hard that she hadn't heard Rachel come in. Her sister lifted the covers on Lori's bed and snuggled up to her back. She'd told Rachel what had happened earlier and thought she'd cried herself dry, but the tears came back with a vengeance when she'd gotten in bed. All alone. As usual.

Her sister whispered, "You're making my soul hurt, Lori. Can I help?"

"Not unless you can find me a new heart. One with a no-breakage guarantee." Lori rolled over and faced Rachel. "I knew this might happen. It's my own fault for getting my hopes up." She tossed her wet tissue onto the nightstand and grabbed three new ones.

"No. It's Deek's fault for giving you hope. And I have half a mind to go over there and tell Annie where she can stick it. Talking to you like that... And maybe I'd tell Deek a thing or two as well. Like, grow a pair. Why aren't you madder at him?"

"I was madder than hell at him all the way home. Thinking he'd just been using me for sex. But then he texted me to be sure I got home safe. And told me he wasn't sleeping with her tonight. That's when I realized he really does care for me. He wasn't just using me as it felt like at first. He's sacrificing his own happiness for his son. So now I'm just unbearably sad. For both of us."

"Maybe you should call him and tell him what a bitch Annie really is."

Lori sighed. "It won't help. I think Deek has made excuses for Annie's lack of compassion for so long, and he'd just make that one more concession. She'll still always be Asher's mother, and that's what Deek thinks Asher needs. He made his choice. Asher. How can I argue with that?"

"For a smart guy, he's being an idiot."

"I agree." Lori almost smiled. "Tonight brought back all those old feelings from when Joe cheated on me. I can't seem to close that door fully."

Rachel snuggled deeper into her pillow. "And Mel betrayed a lifelong friendship. Let's not let her off the hook." Her sister yawned, and her eyes drifted closed.

It made her feel bad for keeping her sister up so late. Rachel needed her rest.

Then her twin whispered, "There might be a way to close the Joe chapter. Maybe you should meet with Mel like she asked?" Rachel reached for Lori's hand. "I'll go with you if you'd like."

Maybe Rachel was right. Had the remorse she'd seen in Mel's eyes been real? It had been bothering her ever since that day. "When I told you about running into Mel, I was sure you'd tell me to tell her to go to hell. But you didn't. Why not?"

"That's what I would've done, but not you." Rachel scooted closer and encased Lori in a hug. "As much as I tease you about being too softhearted, you just are. There's no changing that. But because of it, I think you need to find a way to forgive both Joe and Mel so you can go back to being your happy-go-lucky self. Now please shut up. I need my sleep. And no more crying."

"Fine." Lori sighed. No one could comfort her like her sister. And no one knew her as well either. Maybe she'd set up a meeting. It wasn't as if her heart could be any more broken than it already was. If it'd help her heart heal so she could love again, it'd be worth it.

15

SAYING YOU'RE SORRY ISN'T ALWAYS ENOUGH. BUT SOMETIMES IT'S ALL YA GOT.

Deek walked into the house with Asher in tow after his sleepover. He hadn't told him about Annie. He wanted it to be a surprise. And to also be sure she'd still be there when Asher got home. She'd been pretty angry the night before. And it was like her to just pack her stuff and go when she got like that.

Asher spotted his mother sitting in the kitchen nook, and a huge smile lit up his face. "Mom! What are you doing here?"

Annie looked up from the book she was reading. "I'm here to marry your dad." Then her eyes cut to Deek's.

He had to look away. As he poured himself coffee, he said, "But she picked now for the wedding so she could be here for your birthday too, Ash. Isn't that great?"

"Yeah." He turned back to Annie. "Do you want to come see my room? I've made a bunch of new stuff. Like two dinosaur models and a volcano that really blows up. And maybe we could go to Papa G's tonight? You love that place, right, Mom?"

Annie closed her book and huffed out a breath, but she stood to follow Asher. "Sure. That'd be great."

Deek sipped his coffee as the sounds of Asher going on and on with excitement slowly faded as they climbed the stairs. His son was thrilled to have Annie home. And that was what he'd always wanted. So why did he feel so sick to his stomach?

He took his coffee into the study and sat behind his desk to call up his e-mail. About ten minutes later, Annie walked in and closed the door behind her. He'd been able to avoid her all morning, but it looked like it was show time. "Hey. That was quick."

Annie sat down in the guest chair across from his desk. "I nodded and cooed, so he thinks I approved, but Deek, you buy him too many toys. It's ridiculous. Do you know that the children in Peru that I've met are so poor, they don't have real toys? Just makeshift pieces of junk they make up games with. You're overcompensating for your own childhood."

So now she was going to tell *him* how to be a parent? It took all he had to bite back the angry retort on his lips. "Maybe that's true. But Asher's bright. He needs to build and create things. He doesn't have a TV or a video gaming system in his room like most kids his age."

Annie rolled her eyes. "No. Just a whole arcade he can use whenever he wants."

At the mention of the arcade, thoughts of Lori playing Pac-Man filled his mind. And then the confrontation afterward. He didn't want any more fighting. "He's not allowed in there unless he asks me first. And then it's only for an hour at a time."

"Well, as I was lying in bed *alone* last night, I thought of a plan. What if we start over after we're married? Sell this house that I had no say in, earmark a million dollars in proceeds for the dig, and then use some of the equity to buy something more reasonable? Then maybe I could feel like it was my home too. And not be embarrassed to have my struggling scientist friends over."

That sent a dagger straight through his heart. He'd spent hours designing the perfect home. For them. And he'd paid in cash, so it wasn't like they couldn't afford it. "Why should we have to look like we're something we're not?"

"Why do we have to flaunt our money in other people's faces? I bet Lori loves this house, am I right?"

Annie's question felt like a trap, but he didn't know how to avoid it. "She said she'd never seen anything like it."

"No surprise. She probably took one look and decided you were an easy mark." Annie crossed her arms. "How could you have sold out and slept with someone like her, Deek?"

"How did I sell out?" He wasn't going to deny he'd slept with Lori. He wasn't ashamed of it.

"She's one of those types who used to make fun of people like us in high school. The popular, pretty girls who all ran in a pack and peered down their noses at nerds and geeks. Don't tell me you've forgotten how that feels."

He hadn't forgotten and never would. It was why he tried so hard to be sure Asher never had to endure any of that. "Lori's life hasn't been easy, Annie. You're making ridiculous assumptions. But maybe now is a good time to talk about that dig money. Do you want to go over the terms?"

"Fine. But I don't see why we have to go into it all again. I said I'd marry you. Won't that take care of the rest?"

"Your obvious excitement about getting married is warming my heart, Annie."

Her head jerked back as if he'd slapped her. "Did you just use sarcasm? Or did the world just end?"

"Yes. I did." Weirdly it made him proud. And grateful to Lori. She'd helped him recognize it a little better. "Now how many times a year are you going to agree to come home?"

As they hammered out the terms for the money, Deek's mind kept wandering back to Lori. He hoped she'd be okay.

He missed her already.

Lori parked her car in front of the coffee shop where she was going to meet Mel Saturday afternoon. Tilting her head back, she struggled to hold her eyes open as she put more drops in to help with the redness from crying.

She was a mess. Her head hurt, her eyes were puffy, and her hair didn't want to cooperate. It put her in a dark mood that she was grateful for. She'd probably need it to get through the discussion she wasn't sure she wanted to have. She'd had enough heartache the night before watching Deek choose Annie, but Rachel had been right. Lori needed to find a way to move on, from Deek, Joe, and Mel. Fresh slate and all. Then maybe she'd be ready for a new relationship.

Rachel had asked again if she should come, but Lori was in just the right mood for a battle and didn't need her sister to fight it for her. She stepped out of her car, threw her shoulders back, and reminded herself that no matter what happened, she was the one who'd been wronged. Not the other way around. Mel had better be contrite, or Lori was going to just leave. No use beating a dead horse.

Sounded good anyway. What she really needed to do was channel some of her sister's hard-ass attitude. But then, that wasn't her style and never would be. She was the nice girl who had been finishing last an awful lot lately.

The aroma of sugar and coffee made Lori's stomach tighten with nausea as she entered the café and searched for Mel. Lori spotted her sitting at a table studying her phone. She watched her for a moment, until the flood of warmth from seeing someone she used to love with all her heart passed, then she crossed the busy little café. "Hi."

Mel's head shot up, and then she stood. "Hi. Thanks for meeting me, Lori. I ordered you a latte, the way you used to like. I hope that's okay?" Mel held out a hand toward the chair across from hers.

"Thank you," Lori said as she took a seat. She hadn't noticed how much weight Mel had lost in the dark bistro when they'd run into each other before. And she'd aged a lot in the past two years. Hell, maybe Lori had aged that much too.

Mel sat too and then jumped right in. "First and foremost, I need to apologize to you, Lori. I am truly sick about what I did, and there was no excuse for it." Mel huffed out a breath. "So, where to start, right?"

At least Mel was owning her actions. "We could just cut straight to that night." And maybe get the meeting over with sooner. Lori's stomach wasn't feeling all that great all of a sudden.

Mel shook her head. "No. This started long before that."

"What do you mean?" Lori's heart banged double-time. *Please don't let Mel say that she and Joe had been having an affair for years.* She didn't know if she could take knowing that.

"It starts way back when Joe's family moved into the house next to mine. It was the day I fell instantly in love with him, but he'd barely noticed me. Until my dad died, and because he was brought up by a single mom too, he started to come around more. To ask how I was. We had a special, private bond over our fathers we never told anyone else about."

"That was when you guys were about fifteen, right? Why didn't you ever tell *me* about that bond?" She and Mel had been best friends. They told each other everything.

Their coffee arrived, so Mel thanked the server and then waited until she was gone. "Because he told me the first day of school when I'd just met him, and we were walking home from the bus stop, that he'd met the girl he was going to marry one day. Said she was the prettiest girl he'd ever seen, and on top of it, she was the sweetest. Her name was Lori Caldwell and did I know her?"

"He told me that years later." Lori's eyes stung with tears over the sweet memory. "I'd forgotten that."

"I knew I couldn't ever tell Joe how I felt about him after that. He'd always said you and he were meant to be because what were the chances that he'd move next door to Lori's best friend?"

Lori sipped her cinnamon latte. It was warm and delicious, soothing almost. "Yeah. Joe was always big on fate. And things happening for a reason." She'd almost forgotten that about Joe too. She'd been so busy burying the bad memories that the nice ones had gotten buried too.

"Joe would come over after school sometimes, flop onto my bed, and ask me a million questions about you. He wanted to know everything, all your likes, and dislikes, along with the simple things like what your favorite flowers were, what kind of earrings you liked. Years later, I even helped him pick out your wedding ring, but he made me promise not to tell you. He wanted you to think he did that on his own. It was always so important for him to please you, Lori. He even told me that you two had finally slept together before you did. That's how close he and I were back then."

Lori took another sip from her cup. It was a little unsettling to know those two were that close, and she never knew. "So being my maid of honor was one of the worst days of your life?"

"Yes." Tears formed in Mel's eyes. "But I loved both of you enough to want to go through with it."

And Mel had done it all with a smile. She'd gone above and beyond that day.

Mel added, "I was reminded of how much I still love you when I saw you at the restaurant the other day. I was so happy to see you. I've missed you so much, Lori. But I'm not asking you to forgive me. I still don't forgive me. I just thought if you could hear the whole story, it might help you forgive Joe."

The hardened part of her heart, where she'd sent the love she'd had for Mel and Joe, softened ever so slightly. "So what happened that night, Mel? Why, after so many years of friendship, would you betray me like that?"

Mel took a long drink from her cup as if it contained the courage she searched for. She knew Mel well enough to see all the subtle signs of nerves. The slight twitch in her left eye was always a giveaway.

Finally, Mel laid her cardboard cup down and studied it as she pushed it back and forth between her hands. "I flew into town that day because I had some news I didn't want to tell you over the phone. Bad news. About my health. So when Emily got sick that evening, and you stayed home, I figured I'd come all that way, so I'd tell Joe and then let him tell you later."

Honest concern, coupled with the changes in Mel's appearance, made Lori ask, "What was the bad news?"

She looked up and said, "It was cancer," before she went back to studying her cup again. "They'd only given me a thirty percent chance to live. Being Emily's godmother, I felt you needed to know that I might not be around to take care of her if something happened to you guys, like was our plan."

Lori hated to think of Mel battling cancer. But she still didn't understand. "So how did dinner at the restaurant end up with Joe back in your hotel room?"

Mel shook her head and closed her eyes. "I'd told him about how sick I was during dinner. Joe was upset that he was going to be shipped out in a few days and afraid he'd never see me again. And I was feeling sorry for myself, so I asked if he'd come back with me for a nightcap to talk some more." Mel looked up and met Lori's gaze. "You know how comforting Joe could be. Made you feel like you could do anything if he were on your side?"

Lori nodded. He had been good at that. "What happened next?"

"We'd put a big dent in my mini bar by the time I was drunk enough to confess my feelings for him. And I told him I didn't want to die not knowing what it was like to make love to him."

The picture was forming clearly in Lori's mind. Joe had always loved Mel. He seemed to feel responsible for her, like a brother would. But what they'd done that night had nothing to do with being siblings. "Okay. I get it. You don't have to go on."

Mel's hand shot out, and she covered Lori's. "It was my fault. I was the aggressor. He turned me down, but when I'd cried, he held me until I stopped. Then I think it turned into pity on his part. But afterward, when we both realized what we'd done, Joe sat on the edge of the bed holding his head in his hands and cried because he'd let you down. He told me he had to tell you before he shipped out. That it wasn't fair to you to keep what we'd done a secret."

Joe *had* confessed right away. The moment he'd walked in the door that night after he'd had to take a cab home because he'd been so drunk.

She wanted to get up and leave so badly. Hated seeing the scenario in her mind that Mel had painted. The thought of her and Joe and what they did that night in her hotel room.

And the idea of Joe crying. He never cried. It made her heart ache even worse. "So what was *your* plan? Just ignore that it happened and go on pretending to be my best friend? I would never do that to you, Mel."

"I know." She shook her head. "I felt so awful about it, and I just wanted to spare you the heartache. But I couldn't talk him out of it. He said he'd never lied to you and had to tell you. But I made Joe promise not to tell you about my cancer."

"Why?"

"Because if you knew, you would have eventually forgiven me. That's just the way you are, Lori. And because you are the most loyal person I've ever known, you probably would have insisted you take care of me during my treatments. And I didn't deserve that. I moved back home with my mom during chemo. And then I'd read in the paper that Joe had been killed and I didn't care if I lived anymore. But somehow I did."

So Mel had been grieving too after Joe died. And had punished herself for her crime. That was just so… Mel-like. They both shared an overblown sense of duty to their family and friends.

She'd loved Mel almost as much as she loved Rachel. And like a sister, she probably would have forgiven her eventually. Especially under the circumstances.

Lori took another long sip to give herself time to wrap her head around it all. And suddenly realized how Mel must've felt about Joe. The same as she felt about Deek, and why she refused to fight for him and take away Asher's mother, even though she knew Deek would be happier if she did.

Unobtainable love might be the worst kind of all. It sure felt like it at the moment, anyway. But as hard as that conversation had been to hear, her heart felt a little lighter knowing that Mel and Joe hadn't set out to have an affair.

And maybe she was a step closer to being able to forgive them for making a mistake. Neither had done it to hurt her, that had just been the byproduct. "So, how are you now? Are you better?"

She blinked as if surprised at the question. "Um, I'm in remission at the moment. The doctors won't say I'm well until I pass the five-year mark, but they're cautiously optimistic. Thank you for asking."

"I'm hurt and upset with you, but I don't hate you, Mel. I couldn't ever do that even at my angriest moments. What the hell is wrong with me?"

"You suffer from an affliction called being genuinely nice. And I could tell you'd been crying before you got here. I hope I didn't cause those tears."

She and Mel really did know each other like sisters.

The honest concern in Mel's eyes, and the reminder of the pain of the void in Lori's life that had never been filled since Mel brought on the tears she'd been holding back for Deek. "I broke up with a great guy yesterday. I finally felt like I was going to be able to move on from Joe and find happiness again, but circumstances won't let that happen. Got a few more minutes to hear about it?" If anyone would understand, she now knew it'd be Mel.

Her former best friend smiled for the first time all day. "It just so happens I do. Want another latte, or should we switch to wine?"

"Wine. And cake if they have it. This is a long story. And I haven't forgiven you *all the way*, just to be clear."

"Got it. So tell me about this guy."

Deek sat across from Annie and Asher at Papa G's as they waited for their food. He glanced over to the table where he'd sat last time with Lori and Emily, wishing they'd be there. It was a stupid thing to do, but they came to the restaurant often so that it could've happened. Too bad it hadn't.

It was after that dinner with them that he'd come alive inside again, but he hadn't even realized it then. It felt more like he was making a new friend, not that his heart had found a soulmate. One he'd never be able to talk to again.

It was depressing to think about.

About as depressing as when he and Annie had hammered out all the details for the dig money. They came to a formal agreement they'd both sign after the lawyer drew it up, outlining her visits home. If she broke the terms, the next installment of cash wouldn't come. How sad was it that he'd had to put conditions in because he knew Annie would flake out of her visits home if he didn't? All he could hope for was that by Annie coming home more often, she'd regain a connection with Asher and actually want to come home.

But he still had an even bigger decision to make about Annie. Where was he going to sleep later? It felt wrong to sleep with her, but she was going to be his wife, so he'd better figure it out.

He glanced Annie's way as he sipped his soda. Asher was babbling on about how much he thought he should have a cell phone to her, but she wasn't listening. She was too busy texting with someone. She'd been doing that all day.

He said, "Asher, knock it off. You're not getting a cell phone."

"Geez, Dad. I was just asking."

Deek ran a hand down his face, searching for patience. He'd run out about four hours ago. "I don't want to discuss it anymore tonight, okay?"

"Fine." Asher pouted as he reached out to play with the pepper flake jar.

Deek hated when his son made messes with the condiments, but it was a battle he didn't have the energy to fight. Maybe Annie could be the bad guy for a change.

When the food came, Annie finally laid her phone down. "I haven't had pizza in forever."

As Deek chewed his tomato-y, garlicy, slice of heaven, a retort of *You could have all the pizza you wanted if you'd get your ass home occasionally* wanted to slip out, but he stopped himself.

He was in a foul mood and needed to snap out of it.

Asher said, "We come here a lot, Mom. The last time was with Emily and Mrs. Went."

Annie's eyes slowly rose until she met Deek's gaze. The anger simmering in them was lethal. She said, "About Emily. Maybe you shouldn't play with her anymore, Asher."

His little face fell. "Why not? She's fun."

Annie set down her pizza and wiped her hands on her napkin. "Because Deek and I don't think you should be playing with her, and that's final."

Annie sent Deek a look that warned him not to argue.

"Dad?" Asher turned to Deek with pleading eyes. "I thought you liked Emily and Mrs. Went."

He'd had all he could take of Annie's demands.

He looked her in the eyes and said, "I do like Emily and Mrs. Went." Then he switched his gaze back to his son. "And that's the problem. Your mother is jealous of Mrs. Went and is taking it out on you." He threw his napkin down. "I'll be in the car when you guys are finished."

He stood, grabbed his coat, and walked outside as calmly as he could. He'd rather punch the hell out of something, but that wouldn't solve anything.

After he had slid into the seat, wanting to drive away from his own life, he laid his head on the steering wheel and closed his eyes.

He shouldn't have done that. It'd just send Annie to that quiet, ugly place he hated to see.

Was this the way he was going to spend the rest of his life? Listening to Annie complain about the house, his parenting, and Asher's friends?

Lori believed that she was enough for Emily. Because she loved her daughter and that was all anyone needed, to be loved by somebody. The family dinner he and Asher had crashed at Lori's had been one of the nicest evenings of his life. Was it so wrong to want that for them too? And the way he and Lori could talk and eat without all the game playing Annie did?

Did Annie even love Asher? It made Deek sick to watch Asher beg for Annie's attention like he'd done all day.

Was he making the biggest mistake of his life?

A quiet tap sounded on the window. It was Asher, so Deek popped the locks. After his son had climbed into the backseat, he said, "Mom had to go to the bathroom. She'll be right out."

Deek turned and asked, "Does it make you happy to have mom here, buddy?"

Asher nodded. "Yeah. But when she's here, you yell at me a lot. It scares me that you'll go away too if I make you mad enough. Like Mom did."

Dammit.

"I'm sorry I yelled at you in there. But I'll never leave you, Asher. Because I love you. No matter what."

"Are you mad at Mom?"

"No. I'm mad at myself. For letting things get like this." He grabbed his cell from his coat pocket. He wanted to let his lawyer know that he was going to nix Annie's contract. "But I'm going to fix it right now."

"Do I still get to play with Emily?"

"Yep. I need to fix that too. Just as soon as we get home."

Annie opened the passenger door and slipped inside. "We need to talk, Deek."

"I agree."

They drove in dead silence all the way home. After the garage door had slapped shut behind them, Asher headed for his room, and Deek and Annie headed for the den.

Deek closed the door and then circled behind his desk. He leaned back in his leather chair and crossed his arms. "You first?"

Suspicion clouded Annie's face. "Maybe you'd better go first."

He tapped keys on his computer to wake it up. "I e-mailed the lawyer and told him to forget the contract."

"Why?" Panic filled Annie's eyes. "Because of the Emily thing? Fine. He can play with her, then."

He vowed he'd stay calm. "You shouldn't have done that, but no. It's because Asher told me I yell at him when you're here. Any idea why that would be, Annie?"

She laid her hands on the desk and leaned closer. "How would I know how much you yell at him when I'm not here? That's an illogical question."

"About as illogical as me trying to make this family work. So I'm going to transfer a million dollars into your account right now." He tapped some keys and then turned the screen so she could see. "It's all there. And you're free to do whatever you want to do."

Annie blinked at him as she processed that. "Why?"

"Because I'm tired of trying to make it look like you care for Asher. I'm enough for him because I love him. I'm not so sure you do."

Annie leaned back in the chair and crossed her arms too. "I love my son, Deek. You're the one who wants to make me into some vision of the perfect mother. Asher knows I am what I am."

"Okay. Fine. You can visit anytime you'd like. I'd just appreciate you letting me know in advance. And I'll have the lawyer draw up papers to make it all official that I have sole custody."

"So you don't want to get married?"

Not even a blink of an eye about giving up custody of her son?

"Nope. You only agreed to marriage to get your dig money. So now you have it. You can go back to Peru to whoever that man is you sleep with and have a nice life. That's pretty much what you'd planned to do anyway, right?"

Annie's gaze turned cold. "You hacked my phone?"

So he'd guessed correctly. "No. I didn't. I'm just a trusting idiot who falls prey to people, remember? Horrible people like Lori, who once warned me that I shouldn't let anyone use me for my money. Even if she is Asher's mother."

Annie slowly rose from the chair. "So that's it? We're over? And all I get is a million bucks out of the hundreds of millions you have and a wave goodbye?"

"What? I'm saving you the embarrassment of flaunting all my money in your poor scientist friends' faces."

"More sarcasm. Lori really played a number on you, Deek."

No, Lori showed him what it was like to be with someone who has a heart.

She headed for the door. "We had a common law marriage. You'll hear from my lawyers."

Common law marriage? Probably not when she hadn't lived in the same house as him for years.

He called out to her back, "Or, we could part as friends for Asher's sake. I'll always respect that you're his mother, and that includes helping you with your digs from time to time if we can keep things civil. Please think about that, Annie."

"We'll see." She stopped when she got to the doorway. "I hope you enjoy breaking your son's heart when you explain why I had to leave before his birthday."

Guilt wasn't going to work on him anymore. "I didn't ask you to leave. You're always welcome to stay in a guest room when you visit."

"I'll tell Asher myself, then," Annie said in her typical, emotionless even tone. "Go to hell, Deek."

He'd already been living in it. Nothing new.

He didn't know for sure if Lori cared for him as much as he did for her, but he didn't want to spend the rest of his life wondering if they could've made it work. He just hoped Lori could forgive him for being so damn clueless.

And that he wouldn't be too late.

16

GRAND GESTURES OF LOVE ONLY HAPPENED IN THE MOVIES, RIGHT?

Deek knocked on Lori's front door and reminded him-self to breathe. It was Saturday evening. She might have gone to the movies or something so he should've called first. But he didn't want to say all the things he wanted to say on the phone. Plus, he couldn't wait to see her. He'd missed the hell out of her in the one day that had passed.

When the door swung open, and Lori appeared, he nearly sighed in relief. Thank goodness she was home. But a closer look revealed it wasn't Lori. "Hi, Rachel. Is Lori here?"

"No." Rachel crossed her arms. "She's on a date. What do you want?"

Another guy? So soon? "I wanted to apologize to her."

"Too little, too late, Deek." Rachel started to close the door.

"Wait." He stuck his foot in the way. "I broke things off with Annie tonight. For good. She's on a plane back to Peru tomorrow morning."

The door opened wider, and Rachel's hand fisted in his shirt, tugging him inside. "You get three minutes to convince me you're really over Annie." She slapped the door closed behind them and pointed to the couch.

He moved the drop cloth aside and sat. She stood with her arms crossed and a scowl on her face. "Clock's ticking, Deek. What happened to the idea that Asher needs his mother?"

He opened his mouth to answer, but then Emily appeared. "Hi, Mr. Cooper."

He lifted a hand. "Hey, Emily. How are you?"

"Starving." She looked up at her aunt. "When is Mom getting back from the grocery store?"

Rachel laid her hand on Emily's back and guided her back to the den. "Change of plans we forgot to tell you about. I'll make you something in a minute. Go watch TV."

Rachel came back and said, "Lori went to the grocery store before her date. Had to pick up…beer. Because her date is a famous football player and he likes to play beer pong." She waved a hand. "Anyway, you were saying?"

Beer pong? What the heck? Shaking it off, he said, "I was going to say that I finally figured out that Asher and I deserve to be happy. And Lori makes us happy. Annie doesn't."

"So this is all about you?" She pointed to the door. "Get out!"

"No! You asked about Asher needing his mother. You didn't ask me how I felt about Lori." Rachel could be a very confusing person.

"Okay, then. How do you feel about my sister?"

He stood up, moved in front of Lori's pit bull, and peered down at her. "I love her."

"Because?" She waggled her fingers. "Come on, Deek. Dig deep. She's going to need the reasons why."

Was it Rachel or Lori who needed all the reasons? But he'd clearly not get to Lori without passing her guard dog's tests.

"Because she's pretty both inside and out. She's funny, kind, patient, and am I allowed to say anything about when we're in bed?"

"To her." Rachel shrugged. "I don't particularly want to know those details. Skip that for now and give me more."

More? What else could a guy say? "You mean like how she makes my heart full when we're together, and I miss her when we're apart? And how I never slept with Annie because I feel like I belong to Lori?"

"That last part about belonging to Lori is good." Rachel slowly nodded. "And that's all a great start. But still not enough. You're making the assumption that she loves you back. I think you still have some work to do to make that happen."

His stomach sank. He *was* making that assumption. "So you don't think Lori has strong feelings for me?"

"How would I know, Deek? But just in case, you need to put it all out there and *make* her fall in love with you."

Lori's words when she'd laid her hand on his chest in his bedroom came back to him. She'd said, *"I have to own all this real estate. Listen to your heart, Deek."* He could still feel the warmth of her palm on his skin. "She already owns all my heart."

"Really?" Rachel threw her hands up in the air. "So to prove that, your idea was to knock on her door empty-handed?"

Now he was really confused. "Lori doesn't care about shiny things. She's happy with very little. I like that about her."

"Wow. You are such a…guy. Listen up." She poked him in the shoulder. "All. Women. Like. Shiny. Things. But those shiny things don't have to be diamonds, or expensive. They have to be a token to show love, get it?"

"No." His head hurt.

Man, a vase of flowers was looking awfully good at the moment.

"Okay. Look. Words don't mean jack right now. You have to find a way to mend the damage you did when you pulled that boneheaded thing by choosing Annie over her. What's to stop her from thinking you might do it again?" Rachel grabbed his arm and navigated him toward the door.

"You're right." She said she had trust issues, so he was going to show her he loved her in a way that would leave no doubt that he always would. "I don't know how I'm going to pull this off, but I'm going to do it!"

Rachel took his face in her hands and kissed his cheek. "You really are adorable when you're determined. I can see why Lori fell for you."

"Don't tell her I was here. I'm afraid I'll only get one chance to say I'm sorry, and I need a little time to figure this out. When I'm ready, she'll have no doubts about my love. Thanks, Rachel."

"Welcome." Rachel opened the door for him. "By the way, Deek. How did you know it was me so quickly? Most people have to wait until we speak to tell us apart."

"It's in the eyes." He stopped and faced her. "Lori looks at me like I invented chocolate. You look at me like I'm a guy who wants to break her sister's heart."

"That's because it's such a tender one. So don't do that."

"I won't." He started down the walk, then stopped and turned around. "Lori's not really on a date. Is she?"

Please say no.

Rachel laughed. "No. She was making us her famous Chicken parm but ran out of breadcrumbs. So get out of here before she gets back and sees your empty hands. Don't screw this up, Deek. See ya." She closed the door.

He'd come up with something so awesome, Lori would have no choice but to fall all the way in love with him. He hoped.

What the hell was he going to do?

After their late dinner, and Emily was tucked in bed, Lori put the last of the dishes into the dishwasher and started it. She'd wanted to make Rachel's favorite food as a thank-you. If it hadn't been for her pushy sister talking her into speaking with Mel, she'd still be walking around with all that bottled-up anger and pain.

While the conversation had been hard, it had been so freeing to her heart. As if a weight she'd been carrying around since that horrible night had been lifted. Forgiving them had been the best thing for her soul.

Why hadn't she done it sooner and saved herself all that pain? She'd screwed up there. Now if she could get over the hurt Deek put in her heart, maybe she'd feel like a whole person again. Hopefully soon.

Rachel had a tough shell, but deep down had a heart as gooey as Lori's. Well, maybe not quite as soft, but still tender.

Lori poured herself another glass of wine and then joined her sister on the couch in the den. "What are we watching?" Just once, she'd like to choose what they watched, but oh well.

Rachel sighed. "Two single women feeling sorry for themselves on a Saturday night sound good?"

"Nope." Lori picked up the remote and started searching for something upbeat. "You don't have to sit here and mope, you know. You could call Marcello."

"It's the middle of the night where he is. But you'll be happy to know I told him this afternoon that I had something important to tell him when I see him. He'll be here in a few weeks."

"That's great, Rachel. And it's the right thing to do."

"Yeah. It is." She shrugged. "I hope I can figure out by then how to tell him I love him too."

Lori patted her sister's leg. "You'll figure it out."

"Speaking of figuring things out, just a few weeks ago, you weren't sure if you could ever trust a man enough to get married again. Especially now that Em's in the picture. So maybe this whole thing with Deek was just a physical release, and it worked out for the best?"

Lori stared into her wineglass as she pondered. It didn't feel like it all worked out for the best. She missed Deek so much, it physically hurt. "Deek is the kindest guy I've ever met. I honestly believed he'd never cheat on me. Enough that I think I could've overcome my trust issues for him. If you could've seen the look on Deek's face as he watched me leave. It was...heartbreaking." She sighed. "He didn't want to choose her. He had to."

"What if something changes and you and Deek could be together? It'd be pretty unfair to him if you got all the way to the altar and then got cold feet. You're talking to me here, Lori. I know you struggle with trusting men more than you like to admit." Rachel snatched the remote from Lori's hand and flipped through the channels. "We both do."

Rachel was right. Lori had vowed never to marry again after Joe died. She'd made a bad choice in men like her mother had. She feared it ran in her genes. It was with the passing of time, and the blurring of memories, that she'd eventually decided she didn't want to grow old alone and would try dating again. But that was no reason to get married. "Are you and I going to end up living together until we die? Along with our thirty cats?"

Her sister laughed. "Maybe not if we get our heads out of our butts and work through our issues. And learn to trust ourselves to make good choices."

"I think I made some real progress today on that." She took a deep drink from her glass. "I forgave Joe. And Mel. Mostly. I don't know exactly when during Mel's story, but while I was driving home, I realized he and Mel made a mistake in the heat of an emotional crisis. And people make mistakes."

"Including you and me, and we're too hard on ourselves for it. So you're welcome." Rachel leaned over, and shoulder bumped Lori. "Stick with me, kid, and I'll have you all straightened out in under a week. Guaranteed."

"Oh, guaranteed, huh?" She wished it was that simple. "We'll see about that."

Rachel's expression turned smug. "Yes, we will."

Lori shook her head. Rachel could be so damn sure of herself sometimes. "Speaking of a week, I'm already dreading seeing Deek and Annie next Saturday when I drop Emily off at Asher's party. But I guess I'll have to get used to it. For Emily's sake." She bumped her sister back. "This is the part where you offer to take Emily for me. Because you're my bad-ass sister and would never be intimidated by any situation."

"Can't. Got plans." Rachel stood and stretched her arms above her head. "I'm beat. Thanks for dinner. It was great. I'm starting to get into this eating-for-three biz."

Plans? Rachel had said before dinner she was free to help with the house renovations next weekend. "What are you suddenly doing next Saturday?"

"It's a surprise. One you're going to thank me for. Big-time." She started to walk away but then stopped. "For the next few days, you and I are going to focus on loving ourselves. To stop taking any part of the blame for things others have done to us. To own our decisions, good or bad, and accept we made the best ones we could at the time. Because you know what they say, you can't fall in love until you love yourself. Good night."

"Night, weirdo." Geez. What had gotten into her sister? Must be pregnancy hormones. Lori picked up the remote again and searched for a movie to watch. She'd read the blurbs for fifteen until she found one that looked interesting. It was a classic called *Pretty in Pink*. The description read, *Being from the "wrong side of the tracks" didn't stop Andie from pursuing the guy she liked and going to the prom by herself. So what's stopping you? Fear? Pffshh.*

Fear?

She had her share of that. Was what Rachel said earlier true? When it came to men, was it fear of getting hurt that Lori was afraid of, or was it really the fear of making her own bad choices? She hadn't chosen her cheater father. And after Mel's confession, Lori was sure Joe would've never made that mistake again. He was truly sorry, and he'd loved her, so maybe she hadn't chosen wrong there. And it was just a horrible twist of fate that Joe could never come home so they could've worked things out. Maybe had more kids.

She was a strong, independent woman. She had already proved she could withstand being hurt. A lot. But she did hate to make mistakes. Hated when she fell short of her own high standards. Especially lately, with her slew of over commitments. Maybe she needed to give herself a break. To love herself enough to know that no matter what choice she made or what the world or others did to her, she'd still be just fine.

It was a good plan, so now she was going to do something for herself for a change. Watch a movie of her choice, not Emily's or her sister's, and root for that girl to overcome her fears. And to get her guy.

And when the next Mr. Right came along for her, she'd be ready, and brave enough to get her own guy too. Screw fear. She was ready to fall in love again.

Well, after her heart healed, and she didn't cry every time she thought of Deek, but after that, for sure.

17

VICTORIES RARELY COME CHEAP, BUT BOY, DO THEY TASTE SWEET.

On Friday afternoon, Emily strolled into the kitchen with Asher's birthday present. "Mom, can you help me wrap this?"

"Sure. But I thought you wanted Aunt Rachel to help because she wraps prettier?" Lori refused to be insulted by that. Mostly because it was true. She had no time for perfect corners and symmetrically correct bows.

"I did. But then that Marcello guy called on her computer again, and they started talking in Italian. She told him to wait and then pushed me out of her room. I asked why I couldn't stay because it isn't like I could understand what they were saying anyway. She said because she didn't want me to see anything inappropriate. What does that even mean?"

It probably meant her inappropriate sister was having video-chat sex. At least she was mending fences. "She has adult things to discuss with her boyfriend. That's all. Here. Let's see what we can do with that."

Lori laid the awkward five-sided package on the nook table and wished she'd bought a gift bag while they were at the store. Or that they had bought a present that came in a rectangular box. "Scissors, please, nurse."

Emily giggled and slapped the scissors in Lori's hand. "Asher's going to love this rubber band gun. I hope it'll cheer him up."

"Tape in little strips please." Lori awkwardly rolled the gift in wrapping paper while Emily tore off little pieces of tape and stuck them to the tabletop. "Why is Asher sad?"

"Because his mom went back to Peru so soon."

It couldn't be soon enough for Deek's sake, but she kept that thought to herself. "But I bet he's happy they finally got married, right?" It made her stomach hurt to think of it.

Emily lined up the last of the tape pieces and then shook her head. "Asher said his parents got into a big fight last Saturday night, and then his mom packed her stuff. Must have been right before Mr. Cooper came to see you."

"He was here on Saturday?" Lori's mind raced for reasons Deek hadn't called her since then if he and Annie didn't get married as planned. Maybe they'd just put the marriage off?

"Yeah." Emily stuck her tongue out as she taped the end seams on the gift. "He was talking to Aunt Rachel while you were at the store getting breadcrumbs."

She was going to kill her sister for not telling her. "So, did Asher say his parents were getting married later?"

Emily shook her head. "His mom told him that Mr. Cooper ruined everything, so now they wouldn't get married and she wouldn't ever live with them. It was why she had to leave before his birthday."

Then why the hell hadn't Deek called her? If he'd meant all those things he'd told her, why wasn't he down on his knees and begging for her to come back? Telling her how sorry he was for choosing that user Annie over her?

"I have to go run an errand. Tell my sister when she gets done that she's got a lot of explaining to do and to be prepared to die."

Emily's eyes went wide. "To die? Like daddy did?"

"No. I'm sorry, sweetheart. It's a figure of speech." Lori hugged Emily. What a bad choice of words. She'd never have used them if she weren't so upset. "I just meant that Aunt Rachel is in big trouble with me. I'll be back in a bit, okay?"

"But what about the gift?"

Lori grabbed her purse and dug for her keys. "We'll make Aunt Rachel do it when she's done. Don't bother her unless you're bleeding, understand?"

"No. But fine. Can I have a cookie?" Emily frowned as she tried to finish the wrapping job herself.

"It's too close to dinner."

Emily grumbled, "Who knows how late that'll be now. I'm starving."

"Okay. But just one." She kissed the top of Em's head. "It's Friday pizza night, so ask Aunt Rachel to order it as soon as she's done. I'm sure she'll have worked up an appetite too. Bye."

"I don't know why both of you are acting so grumpy today." Em went back to concentrating on her present.

Yeah, well, Deek was about to see just how grumpy she could be.

She did her best to keep a reasonable rate of speed as she drove to Deek's house. She tried, but couldn't come up with a logical explanation for his behavior, except for one. He'd lied about his feelings for her.

And she and her newfound confidence that she and Rachel had been working on all week were not putting up with that without having a say in the end.

When she arrived at Deek's gate, she poked the call button. Asher's voice rang out. "Who is it?"

Lori took a deep breath to calm her voice. "Mrs. Went. Is your dad home?"

The gate started opening before Asher answered, "He's downstairs being grumpy in his study."

Must be a grump epidemic going around. "Thanks." Lori drove up the long drive and parked under the tall portico. She grabbed her purse and walked to the open front door, while Asher waited for her with a sweet smile on his face.

"Hi, Mrs. Went." Asher closed the door behind her.

"Hey, you. Happy birthday. Emily is looking forward to the party tomorrow."

He nodded. "Me too. See ya." He ran up the stairs and left her standing all alone in the foyer.

Lori walked toward the study and found the door slightly ajar. Should she knock? Or just barge in and blast him with the temper that she'd brewed up on the drive over? Plan B sounded the most satisfying, so she poked the door open and walked inside. Deek had his head inside a Pac- Man machine, and only his fine, jean-clad rear end was visible. She didn't want to scare him and make him hit his head like she'd done when he'd been fixing the pipes in her kitchen, so she cleared her throat. Loudly.

He called out, "Just leave the plate on the desk, Mrs. Tomas."

Mrs. Tomas? That must be the housekeeper he mentioned before. "It's me, Deek. And I need to talk to you. Now!"

His shoulders jerked, and then he hit his head on the top of the machine with a loud thunk. He rubbed it as he turned around. He had his sexy glasses on and a T-shirt that said, *Bad Spellers of The World—Untie!* It was funny, but she refused to laugh. She'd stick to ripping the man a new one.

Still rubbing his head, he said, "Hey, Lori. What are you doing here?" When he dropped his hand, it was covered in blood.

She lurched forward. "I'm here for an explanation. But your head is bleeding. Let me see, please."

He bowed down so she could look at his wound. It didn't look too serious. She dug through her purse and found her travel pack of tissues to stop the bleeding. She pulled the whole stack out. "Why haven't you called me? I heard Annie's been gone almost a week since you broke up with her." She moved his bloody hand on top of the tissues. "Keep pressure on this for a few minutes."

Deek stood and blinked at her through his thick lenses. "I needed to come up with a story to tell you. Rachel looked at my idea on Wednesday and said I needed a Plan B. You're a day early, and there are a few things to work out, but I think I can still show you."

She shook her head. "Why did you go see my sister? And what story?"

Deek looked puzzled. "I never went to see your sister. I wanted to see you."

Lori drew a deep breath for patience. It was Deek, Mr. Literal, after all. "Okay, why did you come to my house last week?"

"Oh. To apologize. But then Rachel said words mean jack, so I needed to do better than that."

Deek stood before her with a bloody hand on top of his head, looking utterly confused and making it very difficult to stay mad at him. But she was willing to make an effort. "So you thought waiting a week, and letting me imagine you and Annie getting married at the courthouse, and sleeping in the same bed this whole time was going to be better than saying, I'm sorry? Or, oh, and guess what? Annie's out of the picture so we can be together again? Well, that plan stank, Deek! Maybe you'd better try some of those jack words on me quick before I really lose it!"

"I didn't know for sure you wanted me to. You never said how you felt about me. So I had to make you fall in love with me. That's what I've been doing all damn week! Do you know how hard it is to do that? I'm no poet, Lori!"

He was right. She hadn't told him that she was falling in love with him. "You've been writing me poems?" She was quickly getting the sense that her anger might be a little premature.

Deek winced. "I tried, but that wasn't my forte. So I wrote you a new Pac- Man game. And if this doesn't do the trick, I have something a little more commercial for you upstairs. I made the game extra hard because you're so good at it. I didn't want you to be bored."

"You wrote me a video game? Because you didn't want me to be bored?" That was pretty sweet of him. But she still wasn't understanding.

He laid a hand on her back and moved her in front of the console. After he had closed the machine up, he pushed some buttons. "I wrote a lot of this on my computer back in college when I was too broke to buy that real machine upstairs. I bought this broken machine and gutted it this week, so it's filled with brand-new electronics. The graphics are out of this world. I just modified the program. So I could tell you a story. You'll get a little more after you beat each level. Kind of like Dungeons and Dragons married to Pac-Man."

He pressed the main button, and a smiling Princess Lori appeared on the screen. Before she began, she asked, "So this is some sort of apology?"

"Yes. Well, no." He lifted his free hand in frustration. "It's my way of saying I'm in love with you, Lori. And hoping by the time you reach the end, you'll be in love with me too."

She studied his eyes, which were slightly bigger than normal behind his glasses. What she saw in them, sincerity, kindness, sweetness, love, all the things that were Deek, made up for his blunder of not calling her. And it gave her the courage to tell him how she felt about him.

She slipped her hands around his neck and said, "Would it ruin everything if I just told you I love you too, Deek?"

"Oh, no you don't. I haven't slept in a week. You're playing this damn game!"

She laughed. "Asher's right. You *are* grumpy." She gave him a quick kiss. "But it's kinda cute. Okay. Here goes."

She quickly did all the tasks on the first level that would've been like level five on the original game. She smiled when she saw she had earned a red-soled shoe along with her points. "That's a nice touch, Deek. And it's probably the closest I'll ever come to owning my own."

He'd snuggled up behind her to watch. And to nibble on her neck a little, but he was careful not to distract her.

"Oh, it gets better than shoes. Keep going."

He had no idea how much she liked fancy shoes, but she continued to the next level. He was right, the graphics were amazing, and the story characters looked just like her, him, Asher and Emily. She'd started out alone, added Emily to her tribe, and then Deek and Asher joined in to help her battle the creatures at the end of each scene to win more shoes for her, special weapons for Deek, and the kids won slices of pizza.

And there was even a bad witch who looked like Annie. Lori especially loved capturing her and throwing her in a dungeon. "You can't ever let Asher play this, Deek." She held up a hand for a high five. "But good job so far."

He returned her hand slap. "No one will ever play this game but you, because of the special part at the end. The grand prize."

She hoped that they could celebrate that upstairs, so she hurried to finish and make that happen. By the time she got to the final level, Deek had depicted a story of the four of them, battling dragons, bad witches, and finally heading up a steep trail to a castle that looked suspiciously like his house, but with turrets added and a moat. But in the front yard was a sign on a post with the words "For Sale" hanging off it like the kind Realtors used. Behind it was a big heart with a keyhole in the middle. The instructions above it said, "Congratulations, Princess Lori. With the help of your loyal tribe, you have won. All of this kingdom belongs to you. Place the magic key you've earned into the lock. When it opens, you will activate the magic spell that can never be broken."

Lori glanced over her shoulder at Deek. "This is incredibly cheesy, but I'm loving it so much." Lori placed her key into the lock, and the heart opened.

Glitter and fairy dust filled the screen and swirled to reveal words that flew by too fast until they settled down to say, "You now own Deek's heart for a hundred years, until the unbreakable spell wears off. After that, it's up to you whether you keep him or trade up for a better geeky wizard. And because you've completed the game in record time, you have earned a timed bonus."

The screen zoomed into the castle, then into a fabulous bedroom, and then to a closet filled with designer shoes and gowns fit for a princess. There was even a shelf filled with glittering tiaras. Lori laid a hand over her heart, which wanted to burst with love for Deek.

She turned around and hugged him. "As geeks go, I think I hit the jackpot. I'll keep you at the end of the spell if it's all the same to you."

His head had stopped bleeding, so he tossed the tissues in the trash and then grabbed her hand, placing it over his heart. "You told me that all this had to belong to you, Lori. And it does. No one else will ever own any of it. And to think it all happened because of a broken science fair project seems like it was fated to this nerd's heart."

Lori blinked at him for a moment. That was something Joe would have said. It couldn't be Joe's spirit... No, that was impossible. "So what do you say, nerd? Want to go upstairs and lock the door?"

"Yes. Because I need to show you Plan B."

She shook her head. "Plan A worked just fine."

"So indulge me, then. Please? And promise you'll accept it because I really would like you to have it." He leaned down and laid his lips on hers, and using his magic moves, shortly had her yearning for more as a warm heat settled into her belly.

She would've said yes to anything at that moment. And she'd love it no matter what it was.

He slowly leaned away and whispered, "So that felt like a yes?"

"Yes. I promise to accept whatever it is. As long as you come with it."

He took her hand and led the way to the stairs. "You don't have any choice. I studied ancient voodoo too. That was a real love spell I used on both of us. Can't you feel it?"

She laughed. "Actually, I can."

She followed him up the stairs as a thought occurred to her. "What if I couldn't have passed a level? Would that mean I wouldn't have won your heart?"

He turned and smiled. "I had complete faith in you."

"Well, thanks. But I suppose since you wrote it, you'd know the override."

"And there's that. But I'm super proud that you didn't have to use it. We need to have that real Pac-Man contest very soon. I think you might be the first one who can legitimately beat me. Maybe."

She smacked the fine rear end that she was following behind. "You can count on it."

When they got to the bedroom, Deek locked the door behind them. Then he opened his nightstand drawer and pulled out a blindfold. "Do you trust me?"

"Yes. I'm all in." Her heart skipped a beat at the prospect of benefiting from more of his research.

After he'd tied the satin strings behind her head, he took her hand and drew her away from the bed and across the room. Maybe it was going to be shower fun and games. That'd work just fine for her.

When they stopped walking, he stood behind her and kissed her neck, and then her earlobe, and then he whipped off the blindfold. "Ta-dah! A closet fit for a real princess."

Lori's jaw dropped. There were sparkling evening gowns, cocktail dresses, shelves filled with designer bags, and rows and rows of the prettiest shoes she'd ever seen. She put her hands together and squeed with joy. "How did you pull this off in under a week?"

Deek slid his arm around her shoulder. "Seems Rachel is what she termed a power shopper. And she assured me she's tried them all on, so fit shouldn't be an issue."

Lori laughed. "Yeah. I bet she had a heyday doing that. And putting a huge dent in your credit card. It's too much, Deek."

"Nope. You promised." He leaned down and kissed her sweetly. "The look on your face just now was priceless."

"Well, thank you. I don't need any of this, but I really love it." She wasn't going to kill her sister anymore. Instead, she'd give her a big hug. "You know, for a guy who claims not to pick up on social clues, you did a really good job with the game. I got the real estate reference and your heart. And my need to have a man who loves me a hundred percent. But Annie in the dungeon was pure genius."

"That one was for me. You were right. She was using me for my money. Something I know you'd never do."

"No." She shook her head. "But I *am* using you for your body." She leaned down and scooped up the blindfold from the floor. "I think maybe I'll use this on you too."

Deek followed her to the bedroom again, and then went back to his nightstand drawer. "I thought maybe we could use this instead." He held up a silky gold rope. "Just like Wonder Woman's."

"Even better." Lori tossed the blindfold over her shoulder and jumped into his arms. After she'd wrapped her legs around his waist, she said, "When should we tell the kids?"

"Tomorrow? After laser tag? It'd be the best birthday gift we could give Asher. He likes you."

"Good. Because Em and I like him too. You, we'll just have to tolerate."

"Really?" Deek wrapped the rope around Lori's waist. "You realize this makes you tell the truth, right? So, let's try this again. Will you only tolerate me, Lori?"

"Yes. Tolerate how happy my heart is now, Deek. Because I love you."

"That's more like it." He dumped her on the bed. "For the record, I love you too."

Deek slowly peeked around the padded pole in the darkened room, his laser in the ready position. All the kids had left after Asher's laser tag party, but they had the room to themselves for another few minutes. They were playing boys against the girls, and Lori and Emily were proving stiffer competition than he and Asher had estimated.

He gave a hand signal to Asher, and his son took off across an open expanse to gain better position while Deek covered him. But Emily popped out of nowhere and tagged Asher, who died a dramatic death. So now it was up to Deek to defend their male honor.

Staying low and near the perimeter, Deek circled to where Emily had been hiding. But when he got there, she was gone. He slowly lifted his head over the soft bunker wall to see if he could find the girls.

"Hasta la vista, baby!" Lori called out before he took two streams to the back. Emily and Lori had ganged up on him.

Clutching his chest, he stood and toppled over the bunker wall and onto the floor.

He opened his eyes to find the girls gloating over his decommissioned body. "That was cold, ladies."

Asher joined them with a wide smile on his face. "That was awesome, you guys. How did you do that?"

Emily grinned. "We'll never tell, right, Mom?"

"Nope." Lori mimicked blowing smoke from the tip of her gun.

He sat up and said, "Well, maybe it's time to tell you and Emily something else, Asher." He glanced Lori's way, and when she nodded, he continued, "Lori and I are dating. Are you guys okay with that?"

Asher and Emily fist bumped. Then Emily said, "About time. Do you know how long we've been trying to get you guys together?"

"What?" Deek and Lori said in unison.

Asher said, "Yeah. We signed up for the same after-school things and even volunteered you guys for the same stuff, but it was like you were both so busy, you never noticed. That's why I moved Em's card at the science fair next to mine, and we left you alone to talk at Papa G's."

Emily nodded. "And why I messed up my plants so that Mr. Cooper would help."

"Hey!" Lori slapped her hands on her hips. "I was feeling awfully guilty about ruining those plants on the drive over, Emily."

"Sorry, Mom." Emily gave Lori a hug, and then Asher did too. "Yeah, sorry Mrs. Went."

Lori smiled. "It all turned out for the best."

Deek lifted his hands. "What about me? Don't I at least get a high five for catching on eventually?"

All three of the ingrates pointed their lasers at him and shot him again.

"Nice." He stood and pulled out Asher's last present from his pocket. "I hope your new phone isn't collateral damage now, Asher."

"Really?" Asher dropped his weapon and hugged Deek. "A phone? Thanks, Dad!"

Emily joined the hug. "Thanks, Mr. Cooper. Now he can stop stealing mine."

Lori said, "I guess I better hug you too. Sorry I shot you, Deek. Twice."

"Way to rub it in." He gave her a quick kiss. "Hey, guys, why don't you go turn all the gear in so we can get going."

After the kids gathered the vests, helmets, and guns and headed out the door, he turned to Lori. "Can you believe they did that? And we didn't even notice?"

"I'm grateful they did." Lori took his hand and weaved their fingers together as they walked to the exit.

"Yeah." He nodded, happier than he'd been in years. "But if we're not careful, they'll be planning our wedding behind our backs next. In Disney World, if Asher has a say."

"It's a little soon for that. We're all in, but the kids need a little time to adjust." Lori smiled. "But just to be safe, maybe we'd better warn them off that idea."

"Or, we could see what they come up with." Deek held the door as Lori walked through ahead of him. He was ready to marry Lori anytime she was.

She glanced over her shoulder. "Just to be clear, Deek, I'm not getting married in Disneyworld."

"A football stadium at halftime? That'd be cool."

She shook her head. "Hard no."

"How about Niagara Falls? I've never been there."

"Too cliché. How about we talk about this in a year. That should give everyone time to get used to things."

"Okay." They caught up with the kids and started for the car. "So, let's say a year has passed and I asked you again, where would you say you'd like to get married?"

"My brother and Shelby got married in Italy last summer, and it was the most beautiful ceremony I've ever seen." She slipped her arm through his. "And where would a princess like me live, Deek?"

"A castle, of course. So you prefer the castle at Disneyland, not world, then?" he said just to frustrate her.

She looked up to the sky as if pleading for help above. "What am I getting myself into here?" Then she turned to him and said, "We'll talk about it next year, okay?"

"Yep." He opened her car door for her. After she was inside, he leaned down to the kids and whispered, "Who wants to go to Italy this summer? They have really cool castles."

"I do!" they both said and raised their hands like good little second graders.

Perfect.

"I hear Lori has always wanted to be married there. So it must be a nice place."

When both the kids' heads whipped toward each other, and they grinned, his job was done.

Rachel had proved to be sneaky too, so between her and the kids, they should be able to pull it off. And make Lori and Em officially part of the family by the end of the summer.

He smiled as he slid behind the wheel of the car.

It was what he'd always wanted for Asher. A whole family. Not the way he'd planned, but sometimes fate and sneaky kids were more powerful than the best laid plans.

ACKNOWLEDGMENTS

First and foremost, thank you to my wonderful readers. You make writing a joy! And many thanks to my family, crit partners, editor Linda Ingmanson and to my agent, Jill Marsal. You all help make my dreams come true.

ABOUT THE AUTHOR

Tamra Baumann became hooked on writing the day she picked up her first Nora Roberts novel from her favorite bookstore. Since then, she's dazzled readers with her own lighthearted love stories, the latest of which is *It Had to Be Them*. She's a Golden Heart winner for Contemporary Series Romance and has also received the Golden Pen Award for Single Title Romance. Born in Monterey, California, Tamra led the nomadic life of a navy brat before finally putting down permanent roots during college. When she's not attending annual Romance Writers of America meetings, this voracious reader can be found playing tennis, traveling, or scouting reality shows for potential character material. Tamra resides with her real-life characters—her husband, two kids, and their allergy-ridden dog—in the sunny Southwest. Visit her online at www.tamrabaumann.com and on Facebook at www.facebook.com/author.tamra.baumann.

ALSO BY TAMRA....

It Had to Be Series

It Had to Be Him

It Had to Be Love

It Had to Be Fate

It Had to Be Them

Matchmaker Series

Matching Mr. Right

Perfectly Ms. Matched

Made in the USA
Columbia, SC
21 September 2017